Gypsy Summer

Gypsy Summer

A Novel

Betty Barclift

Kregel
Publications

Gypsy Summer: A Novel

© 2003 by Betty Barclift

Published by Kregel Publications, a division of Kregel, Inc., P.O. Box 2607, Grand Rapids, MI 49501.

This book is a work of fiction. Names, characters, places, and incidents are either the product of the author's imagination or are used fictitiously. Any resemblance to actual events or locales or persons, living or dead, is entirely coincidental.

Scripture quotations are from the *Holy Bible, New International Version*®. NIV®. © 1973, 1978, 1984 by International Bible Society. Used by permission of Zondervan Publishing House. All rights reserved.

ISBN 0-8254-2038-5

Printed in the United States of America

03 04 05 06 07 / 5 4 3 2 1

Gypsy Summer

Chapter One

Katie Barnes shoved her ten-year-old brother, Alex, through the tent entrance. "Quick, Alex, hide in here!" After a quick peek around the peaceful Puget Sound Campground, she followed him inside.

"Hold it!" Alex skidded to a stop. Moving him now was like shoving against a young circus elephant. "What are we hiding from?" Pushing Katie aside, he poked his head back through the tent flap and looked left, then right. "I don't get it," he said. "There's nothin' out there but a couple of girls coming down the road." He pulled his curly brown head back in and grinned his pumpkin-face grin. "You scared of Washington State kids, Katie?"

"Scared?" hissed Katie. She snatched a handful of Alex's grungy T-shirt and pulled his face close to hers. "You should know by now, Alex Barnes, that I'm not afraid of anyone. Didn't I out arm-wrestle John McGinnis in seventh grade?"

Alex's gaze fell, and he pulled away from her. Katie was glad he didn't seem to realize yet that although she was thirteen, he was nearly as tall as her and outweighed her by twenty pounds.

"I'm not scared," she explained, sitting down on a rolled sleeping bag. "I just don't want to meet any new kids while we're living out here in the woods like this." She looked down at her wrinkled, stained T-shirt and jeans and scrunched up her nose. "And you, Alex—how long have you been wearing that filthy shirt? Three days?"

"Four," he answered proudly. "And I couldn't care less about a couple of stuck-up girls. I'm going back out there."

"Alex . . ." warned Katie.

"Hey, this is a campground," Alex said. "Everyone here is living like us."

Katie shook her head. She shoved her shoulder-length black hair back from her face. "No, the rest of the people here are camping because they're on vacation. In a few days they'll all go home." Katie scratched at a mosquito bite on her bare leg. "We won't."

"Yeah, but we're just as good as any of them. Better than some," Alex said, though he stayed on his sleeping bag.

The two of them sat silently and waited for the girls to pass by their tent. Dad was out gathering dead branches for their campfire that night. Mom and Hannah had gone for a walk around camp. It was a good thing, too; it would be just like their mom to stop those girls and invite them to come meet Katie. She shuddered at the thought.

July sun beat down on the tent's canvas roof. Big drops of sweat rolled down Alex's round red face. The only sound was the distant chopping of wood.

Alex opened his mouth to speak, but Katie grabbed his arm. "Shhhh!"

Katie turned her head to listen. She could hear the faint

sounds of girls talking and giggling nearby. The voices grew louder and nearer. The pair must be passing right by the tent.

Suddenly the talking stopped. All Katie could hear were feet scuffling along the dusty roadway.

"Look, Nichole!" a soft voice said.

Curious, Katie leaned over and pressed one eye against a small tear in the tent wall. She jumped back as two sets of eyes seemed to stare straight at her.

"Did you ever see anything so tacky?" continued the voice. "Daddy saw them setting up camp early this morning. He said they reminded him of the gypsies who used to sneak into town when he was a boy." The petite blonde, dressed in pink shorts and matching top, even had pink pom-poms on the back of her pink ankle socks.

"You know, I bet they've got everything they own tied on top of that old brown van. And did you *see* that girl who ran into the tent?" the taller girl snickered. She brushed back a mane of smooth, shiny brown hair.

The blonde girl nodded. "She looked like a gypsy, all right. Dark skin, stringy black hair, and that pointy nose."

Katie's hands flew to cover her nose.

"Can't you just picture her bent over a crystal ball trying to tell fortunes?" Both girls turned to look back at the tent and giggled.

Katie slumped to the canvas floor. She felt numb all over, like a dentist had jabbed her with a giant needle. Those terrible girls, saying such awful things about her and her family. Gypsies! She had never seen a gypsy, but they must be the scum of the earth. *Those girls meant for me to hear,* she thought. *They knew that I was in the tent.*

Alex breathed loudly, his hands balled into tight fists. "You gonna let 'em get away with that, Katie?"

The numbness left Katie. All she felt was boiling rage. "No way!" She jumped up, shoved the tent flap aside, and looked around. The girls were gone.

Katie began to run down the road. "Hey! Come back here!" she yelled. She tore down the road and rounded a bend, then stopped when she saw that the road ahead of her was empty. They must have gone the other way. She wouldn't find them now. Sighing, she turned and headed back to Alex, who stood watching her.

"We should have stayed in Kansas," he said. "No one back in Sunnydale talked about us that way."

"I know," Katie said. "Sunnydale was the best town in the world." She wiped the sweat from her face. "Everything was different there. But we were different too, Alex. We had a home and a life, like everyone else."

"Hey, we're not homeless gypsies." Alex's voice was getting loud and squeaky. "We're just gonna camp here 'til Dad gets a job and—" He stopped when he saw Mom and Dad coming down the road toward them.

Katie watched her short, wiry mom striding briskly along, her straight black hair glistening in the bright sunshine. Dad was carrying a load of twigs and dried wood on one broad shoulder. He was nearly a head taller than Mom, and he slowed his long legs to keep pace with her.

Five-year-old Hannah danced ahead and waved her small arms like a tiny cheerleader. Her light-brown curls, so like her dad's and brother's, bounced as she moved.

Katie couldn't help thinking how unfair life can be. Why

did Hannah and Alex get their Dad's genes while Katie wound up being the picture of her mom? No one would ever say *those* three looked like gypsies.

"Don't repeat a word of what those girls said to Mom or Dad," Katie said. "They've already got enough to worry about."

"What kind of loser do you think I am?" demanded Alex. "I won't say anything—cross my heart."

His promise lasted until lunchtime. Mom set a big plate of peanut butter and honey sandwiches on the camp table, and Katie helped dish up mugs of tomato soup. No matter how hot the weather, Mom still believed cold sandwiches alone did not make a meal.

They all thanked God for their lunch and the safe trip, and then Dad looked around the table. A grin split his tanned, weathered face. "Did you kids ever see a prettier place?" he said. "All the water and mountains and trees. I can see why folks call Washington the promised land." He rubbed his hands together like he always did when he was excited. "I tell you, God's going to bless us out here. It's been a rough two years since the factory shut down back home, but things are changing. I can feel it."

Their small Kansas farm had supplemented Dad's income as a forklift operator at a factory that manufactured vinyl siding. Then the recession hit. The factory closed, they lost their farm, and now they were living in a tent in Washington.

"The people here seem friendly enough. I met an awfully nice woman while Hannah and I were out walking," added Mom. "She's from a town up north called Bellingham."

"Ha!" said Alex, taking a big slurp of tomato soup.

"Friendly? You should have heard the two girls who walked by our tent this morning. They said our camp is tacky and we look like gypsies!" Katie kicked his leg under the table, but he went right on and told the whole tale anyway.

Katie felt her face growing hot with shame. But Dad just laughed his deep laugh and reached over to ruffle her hair. "Ah, don't be embarrassed about that, Katie. Being gypsies hasn't been so bad."

Little Hannah looked up into Mom's face. "Are we really gypsies, Mommy?"

"Of course not, honey." Katie watched her mother look over at the old brown minivan still heaped high with boxes and bags, then at their stained and dusty tent. "Though I guess after two months of working our way across the country, we may kind of look like it. But don't worry, hon. Dad will find a job, and soon we'll be living in a normal house again like everyone else."

"I can't wait until we have a real home," grumbled Katie. "I hate living in a tent."

Dad's smile faded. "Well, that may take some time. I've heard you need a lot of cash to rent a place around here. We'll have to pay first and last month's rent before we move in. And probably a good-sized damage deposit, too." He shook his head. "No, I expect we'll be living in the tent for a while yet."

"Can't we at least go to a Laundromat to wash our clothes?" begged Katie. "Unlike some people"—she looked over at Alex—"I care about how I smell."

"We'll take care of those clothes first thing tomorrow," promised Mom. "You seem kind of down, Katie. Tell you what, while the rest of us clear up the dishes, why don't you go get some of that pretty stationery Grandma Ross gave you and write her another letter. Tell her how nice it is here."

Katie untangled her legs from the bench and stood up. "Writing Grandma sounds like a good idea." She smiled at her brother. "I know Alex will be happy to help with the dishes."

"Maybe you can put your grandma's mind at ease," Dad said. "She's been doing a lot of worrying about us this summer."

Mom's grim face broke into a smile. "Remember how she tried to sneak her savings into your pocket before we left, Harvey? Mama was so certain we'd end up somewhere out West, homeless and broke."

"It wasn't easy to convince her we'd be OK and didn't need her money," Dad said. "She needs it to fix that old roof. Anyway, God will look after us."

Katie left them talking and crawled back into the stuffy tent. She stepped over to a cardboard box and pawed through a pile of clothes until she pulled out a wooden chest about the size of a shoebox. She lovingly traced her fingers around the hand-carved oak leaves and acorn clusters on the chest lid. Grandma had given the chest to her on the day the family left Sunnydale.

"Since your folks saddled you with your great-grandma's funny, old-fashioned name of Katrina Louise, I think you also deserve her little letter chest," Grandma had said. Katie knew Great-grandma Katrina had kept her soldier boyfriend's love letters in the chest while he was overseas in World War I. Katie wished she could read those letters. But the drawer was now filled with paper, envelopes, and a book of stamps for Katie.

After taking out a sheet of paper and an envelope, Katie slowly closed the lid. She sat on the tent floor and tried to remember. Hadn't Grandma once shown her a secret drawer in the bottom of the chest? It opened with a little lever. She tipped the chest and felt around the bottom. Yes, there it was—a metal lever. Her fingers shook as she pressed it.

Katie almost dropped the chest as she watched a drawer slowly glide open. Something was in it, too. Not yellowed love letters, but money—stacks of hundred-dollar bills were crammed tightly in the shallow drawer. She pulled out the bills and counted them. Twenty. *Why, that's two thousand dollars!* she quickly calculated. Had Great-grandma Katrina left the money there? No, the bills looked too crisp and new. Then she saw a white note, folded and pressed under the bills. She opened the note and squinted to read in the dim light.

> Dear Katie,
> Your folks won't accept money from me so I'm sending this cash with you. You have a good head on your shoulders, girl. If things turn out that your family needs help, give the money to your mom and dad when you think the time is right. Knowing them, that may not be easy.
>
> *Love, Grandma*

"So this money is for us," whispered Katie. "Now, when Dad gets work, we can rent a house. We can . . ." She stopped.

Hadn't her folks just said they could never take Grandma's money? No, this wasn't the time to tell them.

There was a rustling of canvas behind her. Katie's heart leaped to her throat. Who was coming in?

Chapter Two

*K*atie looked over her shoulder. Hannah's tiny figure stood in the doorway. "Hannah, why are you always snooping around?" she said angrily. "Go away!" Katie hurriedly crammed the folded note and money into the secret drawer and closed it.

But Hannah stepped forward. "Is that Grandma's little chest? Can I hold it, Katie? Please?"

"No! This chest belongs to me now. You are never *ever* to touch it."

Hannah popped her thumb into her mouth. "You're mean, Katie. I'm gonna tell Mommy." Slowly she turned and walked away.

"Wait." Katie panicked now. Mom would probably make her let Hannah hold it. She tossed her clothes aside again and buried the chest at the bottom of the clothes box, then jumped up and hurried after her small sister.

"Sorry I was crabby, hon," she said. "But that little chest is the most special thing I own. Understand?"

Hannah's big blue eyes stared at her suspiciously. This wasn't going to be easy.

"Come here." Feeling guilty, Katie laid her arm across her sister's drooping shoulders and led her up behind their tent. She parted some bushes and pointed to the sparkling water and sandy beach of Puget Sound below. "If you'll forget about the chest, we'll walk down there after I finish writing my letter. Dad says the tide's out, and there'll be lots of cool beach. You can take a pail and—"

Hannah's thumb, looking white and wrinkled, popped out of her mouth. "Can I catch a baby crab of my very own?"

"Maybe," Katie said. "Now go wash your face and brush your hair while I write to Grandma."

It was almost four when the two girls started down the path to the beach. Hannah danced ahead, her face a little cleaner and her curls a little less tangled. She swung a yellow plastic pail that had once contained peanut butter.

"Hannah, take my hand." Katie was beginning to regret her generous offer. *We might run into those two snobby girls,* she worried. *If they see my grubby little sister, they'll be sure we're gypsies.*

The trail soon widened into a large parking lot crowded with cars and pickups. Katie's feet slowed. The Barnes family had come down here for a quick look at the beach that morning, but the beach had been nearly empty then. Now there were people swarming everywhere, all of them strangers.

Clutching Hannah's hand even tighter, Katie stopped, suddenly timid. Silently the two of them watched chattering gray and white seagulls swoop low over the water and waddle along on the sand. A sailboat with vivid green and yellow sails danced across the small waves of the Sound. Far out on the horizon, a big gray tanker ship chugged slowly along.

Lifting her head, Katie took two big sniffs of salty sea air. Her worries began to slink away. Boy, wouldn't the kids back in Sunnydale love to be here? "Come on, Hannah, let's take off our shoes. We're going to play!"

They both sat on a huge white driftwood log and pulled off their worn tennis shoes. Katie tucked them under the edge of the log as she saw others doing. Then, hands tightly clasped, they raced across the hard damp sand toward gently foaming waves. Hannah squealed and laughed as cool salt water lapped at her feet and ankles. Finally, too tired to run anymore, they both plopped down on the sand and panted.

"Looky, Katie, here's a tiny water pool," said Hannah.

"Yeah, that's a tide pool," Katie said, remembering last year's science class. She jumped up again. "Let's look. Maybe we'll find your baby crab." The two of them searched several of the tiny saltwater pools but found only bits of clamshells.

Katie knelt on the sand and peered closely at a small round glob. It looked like clear jelly. "Look, Hannah!" She reached a finger toward the glob. "I wonder what it feels like?"

"Don't touch that!" shouted a hoarse voice behind them.

Katie was so shocked, she sat back hard on the sand. Craning her neck, she stared up at a tall, skinny teenage boy who stood with his hands on his hips and a scowl on his face. Score zero for making new friends today. Katie pushed herself to her feet. "And why shouldn't I touch it?" She gave the nosy stranger her fiercest glare.

The boy's sunburned face turned even redder, right up to the roots of his carrot orange hair. He took two steps backward. "Sorry for butting in," he said, "but you were about to touch a jellyfish, and they can sting. I figured I should stop you."

Katie felt her own face getting hot. She glanced down at the round glob. "Oh, uh . . . thanks." Ashamed, she ducked her head and began brushing the sand from her bare legs. "Come on, Hannah, we need to get back to camp."

"You're staying here at the campground?" asked the pushy boy. "Where do you live?"

"We don't live anywhere anymore," piped Hannah loudly. Her bottom lip quivered. "We're just gypsies in a tent."

Katie gave Hannah's little arm a firm squeeze.

"Ouch!" Hannah squealed.

The sunburned stranger grinned down at Hannah. "So you're a gypsy, huh?" He looked from Hannah to Katie, then nodded. "Yeah, I guess *you* could be a gypsy," he said to Katie. "I mean with your dark hair and skin and all. But this little girl with her brown curls and big blue eyes?" He smiled warmly at Hannah. Katie wanted to squeeze her arm again.

"Oh, of course we're not gypsies," Katie said. "We're a perfectly normal family from Sunnydale, Kansas, and we just moved out here to Washington." Katie snatched Hannah's hand and began tugging her toward the sandy path. "And I must say," she blurted, "I'm beginning to wonder why my parents ever decided to come to Washington in the first place."

"Hey, I'm sorry if I hurt your feelings." The boy tagged after them. "Mom always says I have the biggest feet in our family, and I keep stuffing them in my mouth."

Katie darted a look at his feet in their huge blue flip-flops. She covered her mouth with her hand to hide a twitching grin.

The boy quickly shoved a big hand out to her. "Welcome to Washington," he said, smiling warmly. "My name's Tim

Reilly. I live up in Mapleton. It's just a few miles away from here."

Katie had never had a boy offer to shake hands with her before. She felt weird as she took Tim's big hand. "I'm Katie Barnes," she said. "This little pest is my sister, Hannah. I guess I told you about us. Now, we really have to go. Mom will be worrying."

Tim cleared his throat. "Wait a minute, Katie. My church youth group is having a volleyball game down the beach. There'll be a barbecue tonight. It's for anyone in the seventh, eighth, or ninth grade. I expect you're old enough, right?"

"I'll be in the eighth grade this fall, and I'm thirteen years old," Katie said coldly.

Tim groaned. "I did it again, didn't I?" He looked down at his feet. "I guess Mom's right."

Katie shrugged. "Don't worry, Tim. I've made a few mistakes, too. Thanks for inviting me tonight, but I don't think I can come. It's been nice to meet you." She owed him that much.

Tim grinned, shoving his hands into the back pockets of his cutoffs. "OK, Katie Barnes. Maybe I'll meet you again sometime."

"Yeah, I suppose anything can happen," said Katie. *Not very likely, though,* she thought to herself. She watched his tall skinny figure grow smaller and smaller as he trudged down the beach. Then she and Hannah sat back on the driftwood log and put on their shoes.

"Well, I'm glad you're making acquaintances, anyway," said Mom. She patted the bench where she was sitting. "Why don't you come and tell me all about this Tim you met, Katie." Katie sighed deeply and sat down by her mom. Somehow she had to convince her that Tim Reilly wasn't really even an acquaintance, just a busybody she would never see again.

Still, that night as she lay awake in her sleeping bag, she decided she was glad she had met Tim. At least now one person seemed glad they had moved out here. Maybe life was finally on the upswing. Dad would go into Seattle tomorrow and get a good job. They could use the money from Grandma to pay the rent and deposit on a house or an apartment.

There were still a few glitches with this dream, but Katie would worry about them some other time. Pulling her lumpy pillow over her head, she went to sleep.

⌒

Lemon yellow sunlight crept into the tent and woke her the next morning. Katie sat up and sniffed. What was that smell? Hot soapy water and bleach?

The other family members' sleeping bags were empty. Hurriedly she tugged on shorts and a top and crawled outside the tent. "Mom, what are you doing?"

Mom was standing by the camp table, up to her elbows in a tub of hot sudsy water. Calmly, she pulled a dripping T-shirt from the water and began to wring it. "What do you think I'm doing?" she said. "You kids have complained about no clean clothes, so—"

"Mo-om! What'll other campers think, seeing you wash clothes like that? Why can't we go to a Laundromat like everyone else?"

"Laundromats cost money," said Mom. "And this gives me something to do besides sitting around camp all day. I'm going to feel really good when I see these lines strung with clean clothes."

For the first time Katie noticed rope clotheslines strung back and forth between the trees. She slumped down at the table and flopped her head on her arms. "I'll die," she said mournfully. "I'll just die of shame and humiliation."

"No, you won't." Mom pulled another shirt from the hot water. "You'll be too busy. Get yourself a bowl of oatmeal, and sit down by your little sister. When you finish, I'd like you to go get me a couple more buckets of water."

Katie didn't speak. She just rolled her eyes and shuddered. *This is the worst thing that could happen to me,* she thought.

She was wrong.

Chapter Three

*K*atie rinsed her cereal bowl and spoon and then put them away in a wooden box. "Where's Alex when we need him?" she grumbled. "Why can't *he* carry water?"

"'Cause Alex is doggie-sitting." Hannah smiled up at her big sister. Cereal dripped from her chin down onto the front of her T-shirt.

"Doggie-sitting?" Katie raised her eyebrows and looked over at Mom.

Mom nodded. "Some folks camped near here have a little black dog. You know how Alex loves dogs. He was down there like a flash, petting and talking to that pup. The next thing I know, they're letting him walk Trixie around the campground." Mom paused while she wrung out a steamy hot towel. "Poor Alex misses old Mike so much. I feel really bad that we couldn't let him bring his dog when we moved."

Old Mike's better off than we are, Katie thought. *At least he got to stay in Kansas.* Glumly, she picked up two empty plastic buckets and started toward the water pump.

"I'll help you, Katie." Hannah scrambled down from the bench.

Katie looked at Hannah's sticky face. "No thanks, you just stay here and play. I'll manage."

The campground was almost deserted that morning. Not one person was in sight when she stopped under a wooden sign marked WATER.

Katie set one bucket under the faucet and turned on the water full force. Yikes! The water cascaded into the bucket, tipping it over and soaking her feet and bare legs. When she stepped forward to set up the pail, her tennis shoes squished. What a mess. She glanced around furtively. Good. No one had seen her. After the bucket was brimming, she yanked it back and shoved the empty one under the gushing water spicket.

"What in the world are you doing?" asked a voice behind her.

Katie whirled around so fast she tipped the second pail, spilling more icy water over her feet. Gritting her teeth, she set the bucket upright. "What does it look like I'm doing? Taking a cold shower?" she snapped. Then she stared up into the sharp blue eyes of the petite blonde girl who had walked by their tent yesterday. Katie held tightly onto the bucket handle to keep herself from running into the woods and hiding.

The girl laughed, the tinkling laugh Katie remembered so well. "You're the girl camping in the tent down the road, right? That must be fun."

"Fun?" echoed Katie. She lifted one waterlogged shoe and tried to shake out the water.

"Well, look at you, carrying your water, cooking over an open campfire, sleeping in a tent." The girl shivered. "You're just like pioneers." She pointed down the road at a blue and

24

silver motor home the size of a Greyhound bus. "That's our place. All the comforts of home." She sighed. "It's *so* boring. Especially when Nickie had to leave. Nickie's my cousin. She lives in a town near here."

And I bet she's just as rude as you, thought Katie, remembering the two girls' conversation the day before.

She turned off the faucet and reached to pick up both buckets.

The girl was ahead of her. "Here, I'll carry one of those buckets back to your camp for you."

"No thanks, I don't need help." Katie snatched the bucket handle. "Anyway, you probably have to be getting back to your 'boring' motor home."

"Oh, come on," the girl coaxed. She jerked the bucket away, splashing Katie one more time. "I've got nothing else to do. Daddy's off playing golf, and Mommy's still asleep. Anyway, I'm dying to see your little camp."

"You'll be disappointed." Katie started toward the camp without looking back. "We don't shake tambourines, or gaze into crystal balls, or even kidnap babies."

The girl giggled. "You're a real joker, aren't you? By the way, my name's Gwen Van Switt. We're from LA. That's Los Angeles, California, in case you don't know."

"Well, my name is Katie Barnes, and we're from Sunnydale. That's Kansas." Katie was glad her mother wasn't listening to her talking so spitefully to this near stranger. She couldn't help it. Gwen brought out the worst in her. "Are you going back home to LA soon?" she asked hopefully.

Gwen shrugged. "That's up to Daddy. Mommy and I are absolutely bored to tears with all this nature stuff. We're ready to go home today, but we have to wait until Daddy gets tired of the Washington golf courses." She stopped. "Oh, here's your tent."

"Yeah, thanks for the help. I'll take that bucket of water now."

But Gwen was already scurrying up the path to the table where Mom was standing with her hands and arms in sudsy water. "Good morning," Gwen trilled. "You must be Katie's mother. You look so much like her." She set the half-full pail of water onto the table in front of Mom and smiled. "I'm Gwen Van Switt. Katie and I met down by the water faucet this morning, and I'm helping her carry these heavy buckets of water."

"That's very nice of you, Gwen." Mom returned Gwen's smile. "I'm so glad Katie is making friends."

"Oh, we're going to be really good friends," promised the blonde girl. "I love watching you do your laundry by hand like that." She strolled slowly toward the tent. "Would you mind if I take a tiny peek inside?"

Katie plopped her full bucket onto the table and lunged to reach the tent entrance before Gwen could. As usual, she was too late. Gwen shoved back the tent flap and peered inside. "Isn't this cool!" she exclaimed. "Why, hello, there. You must be Katie's sister. What a beautiful little chest you're playing with. Could I—"

With a spurt of energy that would have made Superman proud, Katie shoved into the tent, pushing Gwen aside. "Hannah!"

Hannah sat cross-legged on the floor of the tent with the opened chest on her lap. Sheets of writing paper and envelopes were strewn about the canvas floor.

Hannah looked up innocently. "But you told me to go play, Katie."

"Not with that chest!" shouted Katie. "Didn't I say you were never to touch it, Hannah?" She snatched the chest with shaking hands. She was weak with relief to see the hidden drawer still tightly latched.

"Katie Barnes!" Mom stood in the tent entrance before Gwen, her soapy hands planted on her hips. She had a hard straight line on either side of her mouth. "The idea, talking to your little sister like that! And in front of your guest."

"She's not my guest," mumbled Katie. She got down on her hands and knees and began picking up writing paper and envelopes. She crammed them into the top drawer and slammed the lid shut.

"Mommy!" Hannah ran to her mother and clutched her around the knees. "Katie won't let me play with Grandma's chest."

"Now, honey, that chest was given to Katie. You have no right to touch it unless she says you may." Mom looked over at Katie and frowned. "I'm sure one of these days she'll feel like sharing it."

Mom and Hannah left the tent, but Gwen stayed behind. She eyed the chest greedily. "You're so lucky, Katie. That chest looks like an antique to me. I wish my mother could see it. She adores antiques."

Katie ignored her words. "I think you'd better go now, Gwen," she said. "You can see we have work to do around here." Turning her back on this uninvited visitor, she began tucking the chest away in the cardboard box, underneath her clothes.

"All right, but let's get together again soon." Gwen slowly turned and walked away. "I want us to have lots of fun while we're here in camp."

"What I want," Katie muttered to the empty tent, "is for you to go back home to California, Gwen Van Switt." She shoved the cardboard box behind some suitcases.

If only she could tell Mom and Dad about the money. But they'd force her to send it back to Grandma. And Grandma had left her, Katie, in charge of that money to spend for the family's good. "Use your head," Grandma had written in the note.

"Whew," she sighed. Using your head could be a huge responsibility. She squeezed her eyes tightly shut. "Dear Lord," she prayed, "it looks like I'm going to need your help with this problem. And right away, please. Amen."

When she could no longer hear Gwen's voice, Katie slipped out of the tent. Everything looked normal. Hannah played with a row of fir cones on the grass. The water she and Gwen had brought to camp now steamed in an iron kettle on the fireplace grill.

Her mother looked up. "What a friendly girl Gwen is."

"Friendly? Mom, she's the girl who said we looked like a family of gypsies yesterday."

Her mom shrugged. "Well, I still hope you two can be friends. I know how hard this move is for you, Katie, being a teenager. New friends can make life go smoother."

"Mom, Gwen Van Switt and I are never going to be friends, and she is not making my life go smoother. Besides, her family is going back to California any day now—to LA, where the cool people live."

"Well, as long as she's here, I suggest you try to be nice. Who knows, maybe God put her here so you can help *her*. And that's my lesson for today." Mom smiled and turned back to her makeshift clothesline.

Soon all the lines sagged with wet laundry. Katie decided they looked like waving banners advertising a used car lot. All the campers walking up or down the road turned to look their way. *We look so tacky,* Katie silently mourned. She was about to take a book from her backpack and disappear into the woods to read, when Alex strolled into camp.

"Here, Mom." He held out a small box of red strawberries. "Mrs. Bloom was so glad I walked Trixie, she gave these to me."

"Oh, they look delicious!" Mom sank wearily down onto a bench. She gazed at the handful of berries like they were precious jewels. "I'd nearly forgotten that, this being July, summer fruits are ripening. I guess strawberries must be nearly finished by now." She stooped and opened the small ice chest under the table. "We'll have these berries with our supper tonight. My, how I miss picking and canning fresh fruits and vegetables on our little farm."

Mom looked around at each of her kids' serious faces, then stood. "Well, enough of this talk. Your dad will be back in a few hours, and maybe he'll have a great new job. Wouldn't that be wonderful?"

No one answered her.

The clean clothes had been dried, removed from the clotheslines, and folded by the time the van pulled in that afternoon. Dad shook his head when he stepped out. "No job yet," he said. "Seems like the job recession that hit folks so hard back home is a problem here in Washington, too. Factories like the Boeing airplane plants are layin' folks off instead of hiring." He managed a smile. "No sad faces now, kids. With the good Lord's help, I'll find work any day now. Maybe even tomorrow." He reached down and swung a squealing Hannah up onto his broad shoulders. "Come here, young lady. What do you say after I wash up, we all go for a walk down to the beach?"

Katie's heart felt light again, like someone had lifted a giant bag of cement off of it. Things always seemed better when Dad was home.

That night the family celebrated with a hot dog and marshmallow roast. It was the best evening since their arrival in Washington. When the campfire burned low, red and yellow sparks shot up into the darkness. They reminded Katie of the fireflies back home in Sunnydale.

"Uhhh," Alex groaned happily as he leaned back against a log and patted his round stomach. "Man, this is the life for me. I'm starting to really like this place. I'd just as soon stay here all summer."

"Not here, I'm afraid," said Mom quietly. "This is a state park, you know. Washington State has a rule that campers can only stay ten days at a campground."

Alex sat up straight. "You mean we've gotta pack all this up and move on in a few days?"

"Looks like it, son."

That's just what gypsies do, Katie thought bitterly.

Mom's face was hidden in the shadows, but Katie saw new worry lines creasing Dad's face. Were he and Mom really worrying? Everyone back home knew Dad was a good worker, but he didn't have a college degree or special training. Since jobs were getting scarce out here in Washington, too, maybe Dad wouldn't be able to find work. Maybe they'd go right on living like gypsies the rest of their lives!

Chapter Four

"*H*ow great Thou art. . . . How great Thou art. . . ."

The singing seemed to float over the waters of Puget Sound. Katie shivered. She didn't know if it was from the chilly morning air or the beautiful music. It was hard to believe she was attending church while sitting on a driftwood log on the beach. Seagulls soared over the heads of the song leader and the guitar player.

Alex, who was sitting beside her, gave her a poke in the ribs. "This is better'n a stuffy old church building, huh?" Alex had been the one who noticed the church ad on the camp message board: "Beach summer-church. Everyone welcome. Come as you are and praise the Lord!"

"It'd be great," Katie whispered back, "if only Dad wouldn't sing so loud." Back home, Grandma Ross had always teased Dad that he couldn't "carry a tune in a bucket." Dad would joke that the Bible said to make a joyful noise unto the Lord, and that's what he was doing. Katie glanced around at some of the other visitors. A few of them looked over at Dad, but they were smiling in a friendly sort of way. Maybe the way he sang really didn't matter so much.

". . . Even the wind and the waves obey him," read the college student who was preaching. Everyone was hushed as they looked toward the gently rippling wavelets. After a closing prayer, the service ended. People slowly turned to stroll away or to talk for a minute with their neighbors.

Mom and Dad were visiting with Mr. and Mrs. Bloom. The Blooms had their little dog, Trixie, on a leash. Alex hunkered down and petted Trixie, but his face was long. The Blooms would be pulling out of camp and heading for home right after this service.

"Hi, Katie. Wasn't this a cool service?"

Katie didn't even have to look to know that Gwen Van Switt had found her again. "Well, this is a surprise," she said flatly.

"Yeah, I don't usually go to church, but Daddy's off playing golf and Mom's not feeling well, so . . ." Gwen sounded like she was apologizing. She was dressed all in lavender this morning. She patted her blonde hair and glanced over at the college students. "I'm really glad I came though," she babbled on. "Wasn't that guy who spoke a real hunk?"

"I didn't notice," said Katie, her voice icy. "I was busy listening to what he had to say."

"Oh, Katie." Gwen's laugh tinkled out. "You're so cute!"

Katie clamped her mouth tightly shut and turned to follow her family back to camp.

"Wait, Katie!" Gwen snatched her arm. "Why don't you come to our motor home for lunch? I can microwave us a couple of steak sandwiches. Oh, Mrs. Barnes . . . !" Gwen shoved past Katie and smiled brightly up at Mom. "Please, please, could Katie come to my place for lunch? We're both dying for you to say yes."

Katie shook her head violently, but Mom ignored her signal. "I think that would be very nice, Gwen." Mom returned Gwen's smile. "It was good to see you in the service this morning."

"Oh, this was a real spiritual experience for me," Gwen replied sweetly. "Thank you so much. Come on, Katie." She took Katie's arm again and tugged her toward the road.

"Have fun, Katrina Louise," Alex said with a leer. Katie scowled fiercely at him.

"Katrina Louise? Is that really your name?" Gwen began laughing so hard, she doubled over. "So that's why you're called Katie. But Katie's such an ordinary name. How about Trina?"

"I prefer to be called Katie, if you don't mind," Katie replied through gritted teeth.

"Well, if that's what you want. I just thought since we're friends, maybe I could help."

"We're not—" Katie stopped. What was the use? "Gwen, I'm surprised your family is still camped here. I thought by now you'd be driving back to LA."

"I'm surprised, too," said Gwen. "But Daddy's had two good golf days, so here we are! It hasn't been too boring though." She flicked a speck of dust from her lavender top. "Mom and I've done a lot of shopping with my Aunt Berniece and Nickie." She eyed Katie's faded pants and top. "It looks like you could stand to do a little shopping, too."

Katie held back her answer as they came to Gwen's enormous blue and silver motor home. A sleek white sports car sat parked beside it.

"You brought a car *and* a motor home camping?" Katie gasped.

"We're leasing the car," said Gwen. "We can't just hang around this boring campground for a whole week."

As they walked up to the motor home, Katie saw a shiny steel golf club, bent almost in half, lying on the top step. "Oh, what happened to your dad's golf club?"

Gwen just laughed. "Daddy must have lost at golf this morning." She pushed open the door. "Come on in. This is our home away from home, such as it is," she said. To Katie the motor home looked a lot like Gwen herself—fancy, expensive, and totally out of place at a campground in the woods.

Gwen walked across the room to a man sitting with his back turned to them, a cigarette dangling from his nicotine-stained fingers. "Hello, Daddy. Bad game this morning?" She bent and kissed the top of his bald head.

Her father snorted and buried his face deeper in an issue of *Maxim* magazine. His head and ears had turned beet red.

Gwen giggled. "Poor Daddy. He's not a good loser." She walked into the kitchen area and pulled a brightly colored carton of frozen steak sandwiches from a gleaming stainless steel refrigerator-freezer. Popping them into the microwave oven, she turned to Katie. "What kind of soda pop would you like?" She swung the refrigerator door open wide.

Katie gaped. The shelves looked like a display case in a 7-11 store. "A . . . a . . . anything," she stammered. "Orange, I guess. . . ."

"Daddy," Gwen called over to the silent man. "This is my friend, uh . . . Katie. Her family is camped in a tent down the road."

Mr. Van Switt swung around in his swivel chair. His sulky face reminded Katie of Jeremy Stead's old bulldog, Sadie, back home. "You with the bunch staying in that old brown tent?" he asked harshly. He raised the cigarette to his lips and inhaled deeply.

"That's right." Katie clenched her fists. It was plain to see Gwen's dad didn't have any better manners than his daughter.

He laughed, a phlegmy laugh that turned into a choking cough. "Yeah, I saw your van drive in here. I told Gwennie you reminded me of—"

"Daddy!" scolded Gwen. Her dad stopped, turning his back on them again. "Don't mind Daddy," whispered Gwen. "His bark is a lot worse than his bite."

"Yeah, that's what they used to say about Sadie," Katie whispered back.

"Who?"

"Just thinking out loud."

"What's going on out here?" demanded a shrill voice. "Can't a person get a little rest?"

Katie looked behind Gwen and saw a woman with brassy blonde hair, dark circles under her eyes, and a look of pain and anger on her face.

"Oh, Mommy, I'm sorry we woke you," said Gwen in a little-girl voice. "This is my friend Katie. Remember? She owns that beautiful little carved wooden chest."

Mrs. Van Switt blearily eyed Katie, then looked over at her husband. "The television reception is ghastly in this camp," she complained. "You're going to have to do something about it, Sheldon."

He turned around again. "Yeah, well, these little things wouldn't bother you so much, my dear, if you weren't always nursing a hangover."

"Uh, maybe I'd better be going," Katie said in a low voice to Gwen.

"Oh, you can't," Gwen protested. "This is nothing. Mom and Dad always talk like this to each other." The microwave dinged. "Come on, sit down. Our sandwiches are ready." She pulled them from the microwave and slathered mayonnaise on the thick slices of French bread, just the way Katie liked it. The sandwiches smelled yummy, but the first bite told Katie any meal in this place would taste like cardboard to her.

Remembering all Mom's teaching on good manners, she tried her hardest to eat most of the sandwich. She even managed to swallow two or three spoonfuls of the big bowl of ice cream Gwen dished up for her. Finally, she laid the spoon on the table. "I'm sorry, Gwen, I've got to go."

"OK, I'll see you later." Gwen turned and crossed over to a small desk. She sat down and pulled plastic covers from a computer and monitor. "I think I'll surf the net for a while—maybe e-mail a couple of my friends in LA. Bye, Katie." She waved a limp hand.

"Bye. Thanks for lunch." Katie let herself out the door. By the time she got back to her own camp she was almost running. The old tent had never looked so good.

Alex was sitting at the table by himself. "Hannah talked Mom and Dad into walking over to the swings," he said. "I stayed here so I could write Uncle Andy and ask him about Mike." He dropped his pen onto a blank sheet of paper. "Now I can't think of anything to say." He looked up. "Hey, what'd you have for lunch today, Katie?"

She grinned. "Steak sandwiches, ice cream, and soda."

"Wow, rich people sure know how to eat," Alex said enviously.

"Rich people?" Katie perched on the end of the bench. "Yeah, I guess they're rich. They've got everything anyone could want right there in their motor home. Even wireless Internet. But . . ."

"But what?"

"But they're one of the most miserable families I've ever met. I don't think I saw *one* of them smile while I was there. There's no way they're Christians."

Alex sighed. "But they have steak sandwiches for lunch—not peanut butter. It's just not fair. I mean, look how those people live, then look at Mom and Dad. They're the best Christians I know, but we haven't even got a home anymore, and Dad still hasn't found a job. So how do you figure that, Katie?"

Katie shook her head. "I don't know the answer yet. In ways that really count, though, we're a whole lot richer than Gwen's family—for all their money. Keep remembering that and forget about steak sandwiches."

"I'll try." Alex hiked his heavy legs over the bench. "Right now, I'm gonna take a snooze—maybe I'll dream about steak sandwiches."

That Sunday afternoon was a lazy one. When Hannah got back she was easily talked into taking a nap in the tent. Dad flopped down beside Alex and soon was snoring right along with him.

Mom looked at the two of them and smiled. "It's just like back home, isn't it? Every Sunday afternoon, sure as clockwork, your dad and brother had to have their naps." She brought her Bible out and sat down at the table to read.

Katie decided to write letters. After what happened today, she felt a longing to visit with some real friends—like Abbie and Jenna back home. She crept quietly into the tent to get some writing paper. While she had the little chest out, she checked the secret drawer. Yes, the drawer was still crammed with green bills. As long as they still had the money, she figured things couldn't go too wrong.

Afternoon shadows were long and skinny when Dad suggested that they all take an evening stroll. "How about that trail along the hill crest? We can get a good view of the Sound from there." He squinted up at the sky. "Looks like we'll have a great sunset, too."

Not many visitors were hiking the trail. The whole family sat down on the grass and watched the sun slowly sink below the skyline. It looked like a giant red beach ball perched on the waters.

Finally, Katie stood up and stretched. "I'm heading back to camp." She swatted at her bare arms. "These mosquitoes are eating me up."

"Me, too," Mom said. "Let's build a little campfire and drive these pesky mosquitoes away."

"Are there any marshmallows left?" Alex asked, rubbing his stomach.

As soon as they stepped off the trail into their camp, Katie dashed into the tent to find a long-sleeved shirt. She knelt by her cardboard box and pawed through it until she felt a sweatshirt. She paused. Something didn't feel right. Her fingers worked their way down to the bottom. Where was her chest? With her heart thudding, she flung clothes about until the box was empty. No chest. But it *had* to be here! She'd checked it that very afternoon while Hannah lay asleep in the tent.

Katie leaped to her feet. "Hannah!" she screamed as she ran from the tent. "Where is it?" She grasped Hannah's skinny little arms firmly. "Where did you put it? *Where's my little chest?*"

Chapter Five

"*M*ommy! Mommy!" screeched Hannah. "Katie's hurting me!" She twisted free from Katie's clutches and ran to Mom.

"I didn't touch the chest!" Hannah wailed.

Mom set Hannah on her lap and wiped her tears with a towel. "There, there, honey. Of course you didn't."

"Oh, yes she did!" Katie said. "I know—"

"Katie!" Mom's sharp tone stopped her in midsentence. "You just heard Hannah say she didn't touch the chest. You must have forgotten where you put it. Here . . ." Mom picked up a flashlight from the table. "Let's go back in the tent and look again."

"It won't do any good," grumbled Katie as she followed her mother inside. They searched through each box, each bag, even under the sleeping bags and in every corner. No small wooden chest.

Mom and the flashlight moved outside again. "Maybe it's on the table, or—"

"It's no use, Mom." Katie tried to keep her voice from trembling. She flopped down on a bench. "This afternoon I went into the tent and got some writing paper from the chest. I put the chest back in my clothes box and covered it up. I was real quiet, because Hannah was in there taking her nap."

Katie buried her face in her hands. "It had to be Hannah. No one else would . . . Wait!" She jerked her hands away from her face and jumped up. "No one else but that sneaky Gwen. She was right here last week when I found Hannah playing with the chest. Gwen talks about it every time I see her. *She* must be the thief!" Katie darted around the van and out to the roadway. Her mom and dad both called to her, but she didn't answer. She just kept running, thud, thud, thud along the roadway in the dusky twilight, toward the big blue and silver motor home.

People relaxing around their evening campfires stared as she sped by. "I don't much care what they think," she muttered as she panted down the road.

Her breath came in hard gasps, and she had a cramp in her side when she rounded the bend in the road. *There's the place,* she thought. *Right over there.* She knew this was it. So, where was the motor home? The sleek little white sports car? This had to be the right place. But Katie saw only an empty picnic table, crumpled paper, and cardboard carelessly tossed near the cold fireplace.

"Gwen?" she shouted. "Gwen Van Switt, where are you?"

"Something wrong, young lady?" asked a man's voice behind her.

Katie gave a little squeak of fear and spun around.

"Now, don't get all excited," continued the short, stocky man with a white beard and thick glasses. He walked toward her. "My wife and I were just sitting at our table reading when we saw you run up. Elsie thought I'd better come see if we could help."

Katie saw a woman's figure, silhouetted by a gas lantern on the table behind the man. She relaxed. They looked OK to her. "The people who had the big motor home over there." She pointed. "Where are they?"

"You mean those hoity-toity rich ones?" The man chuckled. "What a family! The man and his wife screamed and yelled at each other all afternoon. About a half hour ago they up and pulled out of camp. He was driving the big motor home. His wife and that spoiled girl followed in the little car. Good riddance, I say." He peered through his thick glasses at Katie. "Uh, they weren't friends of yours, were they?"

"No way," said Katie. "But they took something of mine. Do you know where they were going?"

"Nope. They might be headed back to California, or they might just be looking for another campground near a better golf course." The man chuckled. "Sheldon Van Switt blamed the golf courses because he was a lousy golfer."

He adjusted his glasses and stared down the road. "Here comes someone else." They watched a circle of light that bobbed nearer and nearer to them.

"Katie, is that you?" called Dad's familiar deep voice.

"Oh, Dad, they're gone." Katie couldn't hold back the tears. "Gwen and her folks have left camp for good, and I know they took my chest with them!"

"Now, honey, you've got no proof of that at all." Dad clicked off his flashlight and joined Katie and her friendly helper. He introduced himself and Katie to the bearded man, and the two men stood talking for a few minutes. Finally, the older man turned and went back to his wife, leaving Dad and Katie alone.

"You shouldn't accuse folks of something you can't prove, hon," said Dad quietly. "If your friend really did take the chest, there's not much we can do about it now."

"Gwen's *not* my friend!" Katie's loud protest rose clear to the tops of the tall fir trees along the roadway. "I keep telling all of you that.

"Dad, there's got to be something we can do to catch them. Maybe we can call the state patrol."

Dad took her arm and gently nudged her down the road. "No clues, no evidence, no witnesses, Katie. You'd best just try to forget about it. Besides, I'm afraid that little old writing chest wasn't worth much to anyone but our family." He turned on the flashlight to lead their way down the dark road.

Katie started to say there was two thousand dollars hidden in the secret drawer of the chest, but closed her mouth again. She had the feeling Dad and Mom would be really upset that she had kept the money and now had lost it. The rest of the summer now looked blacker than the sky overhead. Her feet dragged when she spied the glow of their campfire and the triangular outline of the tent.

Mom came out to meet them. "Here, Katie, put on your sweatshirt. Those mosquitoes seem to *like* our campfire smoke."

"Come on, Katie. I got you a marshmallow stick cut and ready for action," called Alex.

"You can sit right here by me, Katie." Hannah patted the bench.

"Thanks, guys, but I'm not very hungry." She looked

around the circle of caring faces, even after the way she'd talked to poor Hannah. She reached for the sweatshirt and tugged it on. "OK, one marshmallow."

As she sat on the picnic bench eating the hot blackened treat, Katie turned and gave her little sister a hug. "Sorry I was so mean to you."

Hannah snuggled closer. "That's OK. You're still my best big sister."

"Thanks," Katie said, smiling at her.

It was harder to smile later when she lay in her sleeping bag and stared up at the canvas roof. What an awful day! If only . . . the words kept ticking through her mind until she longed to turn them off. *There's nothing you can do, silly,* she reminded herself. Dad was right. Just try to forget that the Van Switts were on their way home to Los Angeles, and that her precious chest was getting farther away every minute. Finally, a light clicked on in her head. Maybe they *weren't* on their way to California yet. Maybe they were just heading up the freeway to a campground near a better golf course.

Alex and Hannah were already asleep beside her. She could hear Mom's and Dad's soft voices still talking outside. Katie crawled to the tent entrance. She poked her head out of the tent like a turtle. "Mom and Dad? Didn't you say we have to move on to another campground in a few days?"

"I'm afraid so," replied Dad. "There's a ten-day limit for staying in these state parks. Sorry."

"Oh, that's OK. I'm kinda looking forward to a new campground, anyway."

"You need to try to sleep, Katie," called Mom.

"I will. I think I can sleep now." She pulled her head back

inside the tent and crawled into her musty-smelling sleeping bag. *The first thing I'll do when we get to a new campground,* she silently vowed, *is a camp-by-camp search for a big silver and blue motor home.* "I'll find you, Gwen Van Switt," she whispered. "If it takes me all summer, I'll find you."

Katie woke the next morning when a beam of sunshine poked through a hole in the tent. Everything from yesterday rushed back to her. She searched through her clothes box for clean shorts and a sleeveless top. "There's still a chance I'll get the chest and money back," she reminded herself. "I just can't believe God would let Gwen steal something so important." As she crawled from the tent, she saw that the van was already gone.

"Your Dad's off looking for work," said Mom. "He wanted me to tell you he's praying for you today, Katie. He's sure this'll be a better day than yesterday."

"Thanks, Mom." Katie picked up her backpack and started toward the restroom. "I sure hope so."

⌒

"One good thing did happen yesterday," said Alex later that day. He and Katie were at the table playing a game of checkers. His shaggy curly head was bent over the board as he plotted his next move.

"What?" asked Katie.

"We saw the last of Gwen Van Switt." Alex's hand hovered over the board. "She won't be snooping around here calling us gypsies anymore."

"I'd sure love to see her one more time." Katie scowled down at the checkerboard. "Why don't you make your move, Alex? You know you can take my last three checkers with that king."

"Maybe." Alex grinned. "But Mom said we all have to be extra nice to you today 'cause you're, like, in mourning about Grannie's little old chest."

"Huh! You all must think I'm some fragile flower," scoffed Katie. "Anyway, I've got a feeling I'm going to get my chest back one of these days."

"Yeah? Well, in that case . . ." Alex's grin widened. He picked up his black king. Click-click-click, he jumped Katie's last three red checkers. "See ya later, Katie. I'm off to the beach."

Katie sighed patiently and put the checkers and board away. Brothers!

"I'm proud of you today, Katie," said her mother, sitting down where Alex had been. "I know how much both Grandma and the little chest she gave you mean to you." Mom laid her small metal sewing box on the table. She threaded a needle with blue thread and began stitching up a ripped seam in a pair of Alex's jeans. While Katie watched, Mom propped her Bible open against the sewing box and glanced at it while she sewed.

"Don't you ever get tired of reading your Bible, Mom?" asked Katie. "I mean, I know it's a great book and God's Word and all. But you're *always* reading it."

"No, I don't get tired of reading my Bible. Every time I read it, I find something new. If we search, we can find help with all our problems."

"How about my problem? Is there a verse to help me?"

"Well, let's see." Mom thumbed through the pages. "How about Philippians 4:11: 'I have learned the secret of being content in any and every situation.'"

Katie shrugged. "I don't like that verse so well. I'd like a verse about how God always answers our prayers."

"Well, yes, there are plenty of Scriptures about God answering our prayers," said Mom. "But sometimes. . . ." She dropped her sewing needle and stood up. "Hannah?" she called. "Why are you going down the road?"

Hannah smiled back at them. "To meet Daddy. See? Here he comes."

Mom and Katie started, then hurried after Hannah toward a figure walking slowly toward them.

"Hey, Dad, where's the van?" called out Katie. "How come you're walking?"

"Daddy, Daddy!" Hannah sped ahead, her small arms raised high.

"Sorry, honey," Dad said, looking down at Hannah. He sank wearily down on a stump beside the tent. "Daddy's had a long walk, and he's too tired to swing you up."

"What happened?" demanded Katie and Mom in chorus.

"The van broke down on the freeway going into Seattle." Dad groaned, then loosened the laces on his shoes. "Aaaah, that feels better. I had to have the car towed to the garage about four or five miles from here. Then I walked back to camp."

Mom's face was white. "What's wrong with the van?"

"Looks like the transmission's shot." Dad gave a weak imitation of his usual grin. "The mechanic's a real nice guy. He's getting me a rebuilt one."

"How much is that gonna cost?" blurted Katie.

Dad reached out to Hannah and pulled her onto his big knee. He cleared his throat. "I think it'll take most every cent we've got."

Chapter Six

"*M*an, look at that giant stack of wood Dad split up," said Alex. He picked up an apple and began gnawing away like a beaver at a tree trunk. "It's as tall as I am."

Katie smiled and looked over at the wood. "Yeah, poor Dad. He said he had to do something to keep his hands busy while the van's in the shop." She set a cardboard box on the table and started packing bags and cans of food for their move the next day.

"Well, I'm sure glad it's Wednesday; he can go pick up the van today." Alex took one last bite of apple and tossed the core in a garbage sack. "He's about stripped this campground of dead wood."

"Someone will enjoy all that split-up firewood," said Katie. "But it won't be us. We'll be moving to Seamist Campground." She picked up a heavy can of pork and beans.

"There's something I've been wantin' to ask you, Katie." Alex climbed over one of the benches, sat down, and propped his elbows on the table. He glanced across the road where Mom and Hannah were paying a call on Mrs. Swanson, a hunchbacked old lady who spent her days in a wheelchair.

"Do you really think we're going to move on to Seamist tomorrow?"

"Well, of course we are. Mom called in the reservation on Monday." Katie dropped the heavy can in the box and accidentally squashed her finger. "Ow!" She clutched the finger in agony. "Why'd you ask a dumb question like that?"

"Hey, I just wondered. You know Dad's worrying about how much it's gonna cost to fix the van. Then late last night I heard him and Mom talking, and Dad said we might not be able to afford the fifteen-dollar-a-night camp fee, and . . ." His voice trailed off.

Katie plunged her throbbing finger into a cup of cold water. "You shouldn't be eavesdropping anyway, Alex!" She paced around the table and leaned down to glare into his round face. "What do you think Mom and Dad are going to do? Make us live in our van?"

Alex leaned back from her. "I was just thinkin', that's all."

"Well, stop it. Take my word for it—we're going to set up camp at Seamist tomorrow. The clerk at the registration office told me there's a real nice beach there, too. She said we'll love it." The clerk had also said there were two excellent golf courses near Seamist. It sounded like the very campground where she would find the Van Switts.

"OK, Katie. I'm convinced." Alex managed a weak grin and pushed himself up from the bench. "Anyway, I've gotta go get some stuff done. I promised Mom I'd have her clotheslines down when she got back, and it looks like they're coming."

I wish I could convince myself that easily, thought Katie. The pain in her finger had eased up, so she finished filling the box and reached for a roll of masking tape. She couldn't tell Alex she was as scared as he was. Scared and full of guilt, too. She never should have let that chest and money out of her sight. She ripped off a strip of tape and began to seal the box.

"Wait, Katie!" Mom came hurrying up with Hannah trailing after her. "I want to take two cans of hash and some peas out before you seal that box. We'll have a simple supper tonight."

"OK." Favoring her sore finger, Katie carefully lifted the cans from the box. "How is Mrs. Swanson?"

Mom smiled. "She's getting real joy from this camping trip. I washed her hair and put it up for her. Her husband does the best he can, but some things a woman does better."

"Mama, I wanna pack too," whined Hannah, her limp curls stringing down her face.

Mom brushed the curls back. "All right, hon. Get your drawstring bag and pack your toys."

"My rocks and fir cones, too?" persisted Hannah.

"Of course not. Why do you want to pack rocks and cones?"

"'Cause they're my toys, too."

"Don't be a pest, Hannah," said Katie. "There'll be plenty of rocks and fir cones at Seamist Campground. Right, Mom?"

A little frown puckered Mom's forehead. "Hannah, go pack only the toys you brought with you from home." She gave Hannah a small shove toward the tent.

"I'm really looking forward to this new campground," Katie said. "I mean, we've been here ten days, and it's getting a little boring. Now there'll be a new beach, and new trails, and . . . well, new adventures."

Every trace of Mom's sunny smile fled like a black rain cloud had passed across her face. "Katie, if both you girls talked less and worked more, we'd get packed a lot sooner." Without another word, Mom turned and followed Hannah into the tent.

Katie stared after her mother. "But, Mom, what did I say?" She felt like the dark cloud was hanging over her now. Something was wrong, sure enough. If only Dad would return with the van. He'd drive in with his big happy smile, and everything would be OK again. She could always count on Dad.

But the afternoon yellow was turning into evening gray before Dad returned. The pleasant smell of campfire smoke floated across the whole campground. It blended with the smell of hash bubbling on the grill. The van pulled to a stop at its familiar parking place, and Dad stepped out. He raised his head, sniffed, and rubbed his hands together. "Say, something sure smells good." He picked up a giggling Hannah and swung her over his head.

"So, how did it go?" asked Alex.

Dad held his hand up. "After I wash up and we eat this fine meal, I'll tell you all about it."

The hash, canned peas, and bread and butter disappeared in record time that evening. Dad took time to mop up the last bit of gravy from his plate with a piece of bread, then leaned back. "Well, family, I've got good news and I've got some bad news. Which do you want first?"

"The good news," Alex said.

"Well, the Lord has blessed us mightily today," began Dad. "We got our van back, and it's running great. And, something else good happened as well." Dad smiled and looked around the table. He reached out and took Mom's hand. "I got a job today in Seattle."

"Oh, praise the Lord!" exclaimed Mom.

"Yes!" Alex jumped up on the bench. "Hooray for Dad!"

"Now, wait," cautioned Dad. "This isn't a permanent job. I'll be working in a warehouse—two of them actually. We'll be moving everything from one big warehouse to an even bigger one across the street. There'll be at least a week's work. The boss did say it could turn into a steady job if they like my work."

"Which they will, of course," Mom said.

Katie wasn't convinced. "So what's the bad news, Dad?"

His face turned sober. "The bad news is, the repair bill for the van was even higher than we expected. It just about emptied my billfold. I'm afraid, kids, that we're not going to move on to a new campground tomorrow."

Katie felt like she was on a Ferris wheel, spinning downward really fast.

"Where are we going to stay? A motel?" Alex said. "That'll be cool. Hey, could we get one that has a pool?"

Katie looked closely at Dad's face, then Mom's. "You're not listening, Alex. I don't think that's what Dad's saying."

Her father shook his head. "'Fraid not, son. That would cost even more than camping. The way things are now, we've got money for food and gas for a while, and that's about all. Looks like we'll have to stay in Seattle and sleep in our van at night until I get a paycheck from my new job."

"But where?" asked Alex loudly. "If we can't stay in a park, where *will* we stay at night?"

The supper Katie had just eaten felt like a heavy iron in her stomach. "Dad means we're going to be living on the streets of Seattle."

"That's enough, Katie," said Mom in her sternest voice. "Your dad and I knew this might happen, and now we're all going to make the best of it. God has been with us every minute this summer, and he'll be with us in Seattle." Mom stood up and began scraping the dishes. "We're doing what we think is best. There will be no more talking about it."

Alex kicked Katie's leg under the table. "Told you so," he whispered. Katie's mind was in such a muddle, she couldn't even think of an answer.

No one spoke much the rest of the evening. There were some quiet murmurs as Alex and Dad carried heavy boxes out to the van. Hannah told a bedtime story to her doll in a sing-song voice. Mom sang a verse of "What a Friend We Have in Jesus," but no one joined in like they sometimes did.

Katie sat off by herself in front of the campfire. The sparks shooting up didn't remind her of the fireflies back home tonight. They just looked like dying sparks. Tonight, "back home" seemed too long ago to remember.

One by one the three kids drifted off to the tent for bed. "Don't forget to say your prayers," Mom called after them. She had said that every night as far back as Katie could remember.

As Katie settled down in her familiar sleeping bag, she tried to pray. There were too many things—too many problems. She could only squeeze her eyes tightly shut and whisper, "Oh, God, please give us a miracle tonight. Amen."

If there was a miracle around the next morning, she

couldn't see it. The sky was filled with dark gray clouds. Dad had the van roof carrier all packed and covered with the blue plastic tarp. He tied it down with Mom's clothesline rope, crisscrossed tightly back and forth, back and forth. "Dad wants to make sure no one steals our stuff while we're living on the streets," Katie muttered to Alex.

A drizzly rain floated down as she peered in the small mirror and started brushing her long hair. Ouch! Nothing but tangles and snarls. *Just like my life,* she fumed. Grownups had made all these choices for the kids. Grownups had snarled up their lives, and they couldn't do a thing about it—any more than Katie could get the tangles out of her hair.

Well, there was something she could do about her hair. She angrily tossed the brush back in her backpack, snatched up the pack, and started toward the roadway. She stopped only to reach under the front passenger seat of the van and take something from Mom's sewing box. "I'll be back in a few minutes," she called. No one seemed to be listening. Naturally.

Down in the women's restroom, Katie took out her hairbrush and comb and her mother's sewing scissors. She picked up the first long strand of hair and snipped it off right up to her ears. There, that would show Mom and Dad. She picked up another strand. Snip, snip. It had taken thirteen years to grow her long hair. In five minutes, Katie had chopped it all off.

The bathroom door swung open and a strange woman walked in. She stopped and stared. "Oh, my goodness! What have you done to your hair?" she said, backing out.

Katie turned and peered closely into the mirror. She jumped back like she'd seen a fairytale witch or an ogre. "I look awful!" she yelped to the empty room. "Like I hacked my hair off with pruning shears. And my nose looks bigger than ever!"

She clamped her hands over her nose. "Why did I do this horrible thing to myself?" With trembling hands she stashed the comb, brush, and scissors away in her backpack. "I can't go back and face Mom and Dad. What'll I do?"

All at once a banging sounded on the heavy door. "Katie! Are you there?" Hannah demanded. "Katie, let me in!"

Chapter Seven

"*G*o away, Hannah!" Katie hissed through the crack in the bathroom door.

Tiny Hannah grunted and shoved until she pushed the heavy door open and burst into the room. "Mommy sent me," she said importantly. "You're supposed to come right now." She stared at her sister's shorn hair and her blue eyes widened. "Where'd your hair go?" Then she looked into the wire wastebasket and screamed.

"Hush up! Do you want everyone in the campground to come running?" Katie reached up and smoothed her short hair ends. "I cut my hair, that's all."

Hannah covered her eyes with her hands. "Oh, Katie, what will Mommy say?"

"She probably won't even notice."

"She will," assured Hannah, peeking through her small fingers. "You look weird."

"Well, I guess we'd better go find out, hadn't we?" Katie herded Hannah back outside and followed her.

The first one they saw back at camp was Alex, sitting at the table with his back turned to them. Katie peered over his shoulder and saw he was reading a new comic book.

"Where'd you get that?" she demanded.

"From a trash can," he replied, not looking up. "I found a whole stack of them."

"You know, Alex, someday you'll get in trouble snooping through trash cans."

"Well, it just happens that people throw away lots of good stuff." Alex turned around. "Yikes! Someone scalped my big sister!"

"Be quiet, blabbermouth," whispered Katie.

She was too late. Mom had been dousing the last live coals from their campfire with a pitcher of water. She turned at Alex's words. The pitcher dropped to the ground. "Katrina Louise, what have you done to your beautiful long hair?!"

Wow, Katie thought, *if I wanted a reaction, I'm sure getting it.* She forced a little smile. "I just thought short hair would be easier to take care of this summer." She looked up at Dad, who was still up on the van tying knots. "Well?"

Dad tilted his head back to one side and squinted his eyes thoughtfully. Katie held her breath until he slowly started to grin. "Now that I'm getting used to it, Katie, I think you're prettier than ever." He laughed. "But you gave us a real surprise, girl."

Mom walked toward her, never taking her gaze from Katie's hair. "Hmm, short hair does bring out your cheekbones and eyes. Yes, I think I'll like it when I get used to it. But I'd like to trim those ragged edges for you, Katie."

"Let me see." Alex scrambled to his feet and marched around Katie, his hands thrust in his hip pockets. "Yeah, I guess it's not too ugly," he drawled. Everyone laughed.

"Since we've got that settled," said Dad, "maybe we can get this family on the road pretty soon."

⌒

It was early afternoon when their heavily loaded van eased into the freeway traffic. The freeway lanes heading toward Seattle were solidly lined with cars, trucks, and big lumbering buses. A lot of the travelers looked like vacationers with luggage strapped on top of their cars, campers, and motor homes.

Alex was settled in the far back seat, his nose still buried in his stack of used comic books. Katie and Hannah shared the middle seat. Hannah's head nodded sleepily. Soon she was asleep with her thumb in her mouth. Katie closed her own eyes and tried to rest. In the front seat Mom and Dad talked softly as the van moved along.

Dad was telling Mom some of the special things he'd heard about Seattle. ". . . and there's this huge outdoor market called the Pike Place Market. Farmers sell their fruit and vegetables . . . fishermen bring fresh fish . . . there's all sorts of handmade things."

"Sounds nice," Mom said.

"And there's a fancy restaurant called the Space Needle," Dad went on. "It's shaped like a giant needle with a restaurant rotating on top and an outside elevator. There's the Woodland Park Zoo, museums, and the waterfront. I think the kids will love Seattle."

"Uh-huh," Mom agreed.

She doesn't sound very interested, thought Katie.

"'Course it may take a while." Neither Dad nor Mom had much to say after that.

Katie opened her eyes. She spied an airport and planes on her left, and buildings, lots of buildings—most were gray, like factories and warehouses. The buildings grew taller and closer together. The more buildings there were, the more traffic rushed past. Twice Dad accidentally turned off at the wrong freeway exit, and their van wandered up and down the streets with tall store buildings pressing in on them from both sides.

Finally, Dad gave a sigh of relief. "This looks like the way to the warehouse where I'll be working." They drove under several freeway overpasses and turned into an area of weedy lots and rundown warehouses.

"There!" Dad pointed at a building with peeling yellow paint. "That's it." He pointed to a bigger cement building across the street. "That's where we'll be moving things."

"I hope that place can afford to pay you," said Mom.

"Don't worry about that," said Dad. "You ought to see all the expensive equipment inside the old warehouse." Katie began to see an apartment building now and then and finally a few clusters of homes, mostly older ones. A supermarket. A strip mall. A used car lot. Dad drove slower. "I expect we'll headquarter around here somewhere," he said. He circled a few more blocks and a small city park came into sight.

"Why don't we stop here for a while?" Mom suggested. "It'll help us pass the afternoon." It was a nice little park. They all felt glad to get outside when Dad pulled into the small parking lot. The remainder of the afternoon went quickly. There was a Little League softball game to watch, comfortable benches to sit on, a drinking fountain, and clean restrooms.

"Why don't we put our tent up here and stay?" asked Hannah.

"'Fraid we can't, honey," said Dad. "This is just a day-use park. They close everything up at night."

The family ate the lunch Mom had fixed before they left camp and climbed back into the van. The sun had gone down, and it was getting darker.

Alex poked Katie gently on the back. "I wonder where we'll sleep tonight," he whispered.

Katie shrugged. "I read an article about homeless people who slept in the doorways of stores at night."

"You're kiddin', aren't you?" his voice squeaked.

"Of course I'm kidding. We're staying at the Ritz Hotel, hadn't you heard?" Katie stopped herself. Whenever she was worried or afraid, she was apt to start being sarcastic or even rude. No use picking on Alex. This wasn't his fault. It really wasn't anyone's fault.

Alex sat back and folded his arms. "I'm not talking to you anymore," he said.

A huge, well-lit supermarket stood just ahead, and Mom decided to run in for a few groceries. "I'll go by myself this time." She looked in the back seats. "No one's going to talk me into buying junk food." Alex and Hannah groaned.

As they waited in the van, Dad tapped his fingers restlessly against the steering wheel. At last Mom came back with bread, cheese, and a quart of milk. Then Dad slowly steered the van around to the rear of the big parking lot. The lights were dimmer back here. Several huge dumpsters sat lined up against the store. The parking lot was enclosed in high chain-link fencing. The shadowy limbs from a scraggly tree leaned over the fence.

Dad pulled up beside the fence and turned off the van. "How about this?" he asked. "There's some light for safety, and we shouldn't be in anyone's way out here."

Mom agreed that it seemed a practical place to park. "But let's be sure all the doors are locked," she cautioned. "Alex, climb in the back end and get out the pillows and blankets I left there."

"Remember," said Dad, "we're only roughing it out here for a few nights, guys. There are folks sleeping on the streets tonight who don't have the hope of anything better."

"Yeah," replied Katie. "I hope none of them try to break into our van."

"Will they hurt us?" asked Hannah anxiously.

"No one is going to bother us, honey," assured Mom. She frowned back at Katie. "Now let's all say our prayers and get some sleep. Dad has work tomorrow."

I won't close my eyes tonight, Katie silently vowed. There were noises all around in the darkness. Distant shouting, cars honking, and engines backfiring. Sirens. Probably God couldn't even hear their prayers.

Gradually, Katie heard the sounds of deep breathing and snores as everyone settled into uncomfortable sleep.

I'll just close my eyelids for a second, thought Katie. They feel so heavy. . . . The night sounds were growing fainter. . . .

Splat! Katie jerked awake at the loud squishy sound.

"What was that?" Dad and Mom shouted in unison.

Katie's heart was beating hard. "I . . . I th-think someone threw something and hit our window." She reached back to yank Alex's blanket. "Alex, did you see?" She sat up straight. No one was under the blanket! "Alex is gone! He's not in the van!"

"What?" Dad swung open the door and started to step out. Just then there was a creak. The door beside Katie slid open. A panting Alex awkwardly clambered inside with something in his arms.

"Start driving, Dad," he shouted. "Let's get out of here, quick!"

"What's going on, son?" demanded Dad as he sat back down.

Alex shoved the rear door shut and locked it. "I'll tell you later, Dad, but we gotta go! There's a crazy old man after me. He might hurt someone."

Dad turned on the motor and drove around to the lighted front part of the grocery store. Then he stopped and leaned over the front seat. "All right, son, what have you been up to?"

"Hey, I didn't do anything wrong," protested Alex. "I woke up and saw a clerk come out back and dump a whole boxful of bananas in the big dumpster. I got to thinking how good those bananas would taste if they were still kinda fresh, so I slipped out to get a few."

"You *stole* bananas?" Mom gasped.

"Oh, no—they threw 'em away. I just decided to recycle a few. Look!" He held up a bunch of yellow bananas flecked with tiny black spots. "I remembered how you always told us not to waste things, Mom."

"So how come someone's chasing you?" Katie nervously looked out the window.

"An old bum was sleeping in the dumpster. When I climbed in, he started yelling and chasing me, saying I had no right to be there. He was throwing things, too. Man, he was nuts."

"It looks like a rotten tomato hit our window," said Katie. "I told you you'd get into trouble for snooping around in garbage cans, Alex."

Mom held her head like she had a migraine headache. "Alex Barnes, I'm ashamed of you. The poor man probably had no other place to sleep but that dumpster. You must have scared him half to death." She shook her head. "Young man, you are not to leave this van again unless you check with your dad or me. Is that clear?"

"Yes, Mom," agreed a meek Alex.

Dad started up the motor once more. "It seems we have to find another place to spend the night." He began backing around. "I don't think Alex's new acquaintance will want us to stay here." Even though the night was late, they had to drive ten blocks before finding a dark, quiet side street.

"Look!" Mom pointed across the street. "There's a church. Surely Christians won't care if we spend the rest of the night in their parking lot."

"Right." Dad pulled in and guided the van to the back of the church parking area. "I'm sure they won't mind." He shut off the motor and leaned his head back wearily. "We'll be out of here early, anyway."

Hannah's big eyes looked bigger than ever in the darkness. "Do we have to say our prayers again?" she asked Katie.

Katie laughed softly. "It wouldn't hurt." This seemed like a lot better place to pray than behind a dumpster at a grocery store. Soon Hannah's tangled curls rested against Katie's shoulder. Katie leaned her own head back and almost instantly dropped off to sleep.

At first she thought the bright light shining into their van was part of a dream. Then she heard Mom's window begin to roll down, and she realized the bright light was a flashlight beam.

Chapter Eight

*K*atie jerked back from the window, but not before she'd seen a man's face pressed close to stare in at her. The man turned and aimed his blinding flashlight beam at Mom in the front seat.

"Did you people sleep here in our church parking lot last night?" he demanded.

"Yes, we did." Mom rolled her window down further and shielded her eyes against the glaring light. "We sure do thank the good folks of this church for a safe place to park last night. You see—"

"Well, this is not a campground. You can't stay here." The man puffed his chest out until his white shirt gleamed against his black suit. Katie thought he looked just like a penguin. "I happen to be Reverend Drew Lawrence, minister of this church," he said proudly. "Fortunately, I stopped by on my way across the state to a seminar." Finally, he clicked off the flashlight. "Of course, we want to do our Christian duty, but if we let one of you homeless families stay on the church grounds we'll be besieged by all the homeless in Seattle."

By now Dad was awake, too. He hastily ran his fingers

through his thick curly hair and reached in his back pocket for the keys. "I'm really sorry if we bothered anyone by staying here," he said. "We just hoped, this being a house of God, that maybe you wouldn't mind for one night if . . ." His words trailed off as the minister pointed toward the street.

"There are missions down in the central area of Seattle. I'm sure they'll be glad to help you." Reverend Lawrence turned and waddled importantly toward his neat brick church building.

"Mom, tell that man we're not street people!" said Katie angrily. But Mom only rolled up her window. Katie tugged at the back of Dad's car seat. "Dad, tell that so-called minister we're not poor trash looking for a handout. Why, you've got a job here in Seattle. Don't let him talk to us like that." But the only sound was the coughing rumble of the van's motor. *Being homeless does something awful to grown-ups,* she thought sadly. *I'll never let that happen to me.*

The morning sun was trying to peek over the tops of the drab buildings as they rode along the quiet streets. When they came to the little city park, Dad pulled up and parked beside it. Across the street was a row of houses, but the windows were dark. People were still curled up in their beds.

"The park restrooms here won't be open yet," said Mom. She stepped outside. "We can at least eat breakfast at a picnic table, and I'll fix your dad's lunch for work."

All three children shivered and sat down on the dew-damp bench. Katie's arms were all goose-pimply. The back of her neck felt cold, reminding her that only the day before, she had cut off her long hair. Funny, it seemed more like a week ago. She was glad she'd done it, though. Now it wouldn't matter whether she combed her hair or not.

Hannah sat across from Katie with her thumb in her mouth. "Why was that man so mean, Mommy?"

"He just didn't know us, honey," replied Mom. "Sometimes people are afraid of other folks when they don't know them." She smoothed Hannah's tangled curls. "It will be different when we've been here awhile."

Oh, sure, thought Katie. She watched Mom smear margarine and mustard on bread slices, then add cheese.

More cars were traveling up and down the city streets when it was time for Dad to go to his new job. Mom moved into the driver's seat of the van. "If I'll be driving you kids around after we leave your dad, I need to learn these Seattle streets." Cautiously, she looked both ways before guiding the van into a lane of traffic. "I doubt I'll ever be arrested for speeding," she joked as the van moved slowly along.

"Why don't we just stay here and let Dad take the van?" asked Alex. "It's not like we'll be goin' anywhere."

Dad shook his head. "I couldn't leave my family in this city with no shelter at all. It's bad enough to have no home for you."

"Now, don't talk that way, Harvey," said Mom. "This is real temporary for us, remember?"

Dad's words came back to Katie when they drove by a small strip mall. She saw two men curled up on the bare sidewalk by a store entrance. One of the men was wrapped in a sleeping bag. His companion was warmed only by a thin jacket. Katie shivered even though the car heater was on.

Before long, guided by Dad's careful directions, they

reached the warehouse district and pulled up by the old yel-low building with the sign Washington Grocers Association. Soon Dad climbed out of the van and joined a line of men trudging into the big ramshackle building.

Katie climbed into the front seat beside her mother. "Let's go visit some of the sights of Seattle, like the Space Needle," she suggested hopefully. "It seems like all we've seen are the ugly back streets."

"There'll be plenty of time for sight-seeing after we start living like normal folks again," said Mom. "Today I'm just concerned about looking after you three kids, and picking your dad up from work."

"Mommy, I need to go potty," piped Hannah.

"I'm sorry, but you'll have to wait, honey." Mom anxiously peered out at the overhead traffic lights. "The park's restrooms don't open until eight, and it's not quite seven yet."

"But I need to go now!" Hannah's voice got shriller.

Mom sighed and clutched the steering wheel tighter. "All right, kids. Watch for a service station that's open."

After two more blocks, Hannah was wriggling in her seat. "Mommy!" she whimpered.

"There's a station." Katie pointed across the street. "It's an awful-looking old place, though."

"It'll do." Mom moved to the left lane. There were no bright lights above this station. Only a single glaring bulb illumi-nated the faded words, "Sam's Super Station." Mom pulled the van around to the back and stopped. "Katie, rush Hannah into the restroom while I park."

"Katie do this, Katie do that," grumbled Katie under her

breath. She took Hannah to a small door with crooked lettering that read, "Ladies." Reaching in and turning on the light switch, she shoved her small sister into the room.

"It's dirty and scary in here," complained Hannah.

Katie poked her head inside the room. "Yuk," she agreed. "Here, let's cover the seat with toilet paper. Now hurry, and remember to wash your hands really well."

Minutes later, they dashed back to the van.

"Hey, you kids!" yelled a harsh voice. Looking back, Katie saw a white-haired old man in greasy coveralls chasing after them. His dark red face was twisted with rage. "Them restrooms aren't for just anyone. They're for my cash customers, which you two sure ain't. Now, git!"

"Run, Hannah!" shouted Katie. They sped around the corner to Mom and the van. Safely inside, her words tumbled over each other as she told about the horribly dirty restroom and the even more horrible old man who had chased them away. "Let's go," she pleaded.

Instead, Mom opened the van door and stepped outside. "I think I'll have a few words with that man."

"Mom, what are you doing?" gasped Katie.

"You three wait here with the doors locked. I'll be back in a few minutes." Mom's back was very straight as she marched up to the station.

Katie, Alex, and Hannah sat as motionless as ice statues and watched her. They saw Mom shove the door open and go inside. They saw her head bob up and down while she talked. They saw the old man's head jerk when he talked back. Finally, they saw Mom shake her finger right in the man's face. He backed off.

70

Katie collapsed against the seat and grinned. "We can relax, guys. It looks like Mom's got her old spunk back." Mom strode back to the van wearing a smile.

"Did you tell that old guy off, Mom?" asked Alex eagerly.

"Sam and I have an agreement," said Mom.

"What kind of agreement?" demanded Katie.

Mom didn't answer. She just went around and opened the back of the van. Hunting through the packed boxes, she pulled out a plastic mop bucket, detergent, and bleach. "Come on, kids. We're going to clean Sam's restrooms like they've never been scrubbed before."

"That's the agreement you made with Sam?" howled Katie. "He throws a tantrum just because we used his filthy old restroom, and now we're going to clean two of them for him? What kind of agreement is that?"

"A good one," replied Mom. "First of all, we're helping someone in need. It's plain to see the poor, ornery old man can't afford to pay someone to clean this place. And, secondly"—she motioned for them to follow her—"Sam has agreed that in return, we can stop by any time we need to use his restrooms. After this morning, I think you'll agree that will come in handy."

Katie sat mute for a few minutes, then slowly slid the back door of the van open and stepped out.

"Come on, kids. It will be nice to be able to stop by and use clean restrooms—maybe even brush our teeth in the morning."

Dust and grime flew at Sam's Super Station that morning. The Barneses swept dirt from the floors, and cobwebs and bugs from the walls and ceilings. They scrubbed the ancient fixtures, tossed out crumpled paper towels, and emptied bucket after bucket of greasy black water. It was past noon when Mom brought Sam out to inspect their work. He scowled fiercely as he walked toward them, his hands crammed into the pockets of his filthy coveralls.

Silently, he looked in the spotless women's restroom. Turning, he strode over to the men's room and inspected every corner. Finally, he nodded his head and cleared his raspy throat. "Not bad. Not bad at all," he said. "'Course, I expect you'll be comin' back a dozen times a day, usin' these restrooms when my customers need 'em."

Alex nudged Katie. "There's only been one customer in here so far today," he muttered out of the corner of his mouth. Katie snickered.

"Oh, I don't think we'll need to stop by that often, Sam," said Mom. "But I'm sure you'll remember our agreement whenever we do come by."

Sam's red face got dark. "Now, lady, my word is my bond. Just make sure you leave these restrooms as clean as they are now." He turned and went inside his station.

"What a rotten old man," fumed Katie. "Not one word of thanks for all we did for him."

"Oh, he's thankful," replied Mom. "He just doesn't know how to show it. Now, let's get washed up and change clothes. We'll go back to the park and eat lunch." Katie decided the afternoon couldn't help but be better than the morning. She changed into her favorite purple T-shirt, ran a comb through her short, shaggy hair, and brushed her teeth. As soon as they ate lunch, she planned to spend the afternoon resting.

The park was crowded, but they managed to find a spot

under a spindly maple tree. Mom spread a blanket, and they soon had a lunch of peanut butter sandwiches, lukewarm Kool-Aid, and the last of the very ripe bananas.

After stuffing himself, Alex yawned, stretched out on the blanket, and read comic books. As usual, Hannah begged and coaxed until Mom took her for a walk over by the swings.

Katie wearily sat with her back against the tree trunk. She stretched out her legs, folded her arms, and closed her eyes. The street noises and voices in the park faded.

"Ouch!" Her eyes flew open when she felt a sharp pain on her legs. She looked down, saw smoldering cigarette ashes scattered over her bare legs, and quickly brushed them off.

Furious, Katie stared up into the leering faces of three teenage boys. One of them held a half-smoked cigarette between two fingers. "Watch where you flick your ashes," snarled Katie.

"Yeah? Says who?" taunted the boy. He held the cigarette over her legs again. His skin had a pale waxy look, and dirty blond hair hung in strings down to his shoulders.

"I say so!" Katie leaped to her feet, snatched the cigarette, threw it to the ground, and stomped it. "There!"

"Why, you . . ." The boy grabbed her arm and twisted it until she squealed with pain.

"Hey, Ringo, don't let her get to you, man! She's just a dumb girl." The second boy, a tall African-American, took his friend's arm and hauled him away down the sidewalk. The third, who looked to be either Vietnamese- or Chinese-American, tagged silently after them.

Ringo pulled away and looked back at Katie. "I'll be meeting up with you again, girlie," he vowed. "That's a promise." Anger had turned his pale eyes black.

Chapter Nine

"*M*an, you'd better watch out for those guys, Katie! You really made 'em mad." Alex had reared up on the blanket to stare after Ringo and his followers.

"Oh, right," scoffed Katie.

"What guys?" demanded a stern voice behind them. Katie turned to see Mom and Hannah, back from the swings.

"Hi, Mom. Uh, did you two have fun?"

"Don't change the subject, Katie." Mom took a hairbrush from her bag and began brushing Hannah's tangled curls. "Who was Alex talking about?"

Katie shrugged. "Oh, three jerks walked by acting creepy." She reached down and tenderly rubbed the red spot on her leg.

After hearing the story, Mom shuddered. "Those boys were rude, for sure, but they were also dangerous. They could have hurt you badly. Katie, you *must* learn to control that hot temper." Mom sighed, stashed the brush away, and gave Hannah a gentle shove toward the van. "I think we'd better go somewhere else for the afternoon. I noticed a big Lowe's hardware store a couple of blocks from here." Before Katie and

Alex had a chance to gripe, they'd been hustled into the van and were headed down the street once more.

"This is your fault, Katie," Alex hissed in her ear. "We could be back at the park enjoying ourselves if it wasn't for your temper."

"Ha!" Katie whispered back. "Well, if you hadn't been climbing in dumpsters after dark and scaring poor old men, we'd all have gotten a good night's sleep last night." She scowled at Alex. "Anyway, looking at screws and bolts for a while won't hurt you."

Alex sighed.

⌒

That afternoon when they picked Dad up at work, he took a glance at their hot sweaty faces and chuckled. "It looks like you four had a tougher day than I did."

Katie thought back on the three bullies who had harassed her. She thought of the hours of walking down long store aisles looking at boring screws and nails and tools and lumber. "Dad, you'll never know."

"What do you say we go to a nice air-conditioned hamburger place, and you tell me all about it?" he said.

"Can we afford—" began Mom, then she stopped, wearily rested her head against the back of the seat, and closed her eyes. "That sounds wonderful."

The minute they stepped into Hamie's Burgers, Alex marched straight up to the order counter. "Let's see. I'll have a number-four meal with the extra-large fries, and—"

Mom nudged him to one side. "Cancel that order," she

said to the gawky teenage clerk. "We'll each have a sixty-nine cent cheeseburger. Make that two cheeseburgers for my husband, and one large order of fries. And ice water to drink, please."

"Just ice water?" The clerk raised his blond eyebrows clear up to the roots of his dyed pink and blue hair while he pecked out their order on a computer.

"Mom, please!" moaned Katie. Did her mom want the whole world to know how poor they were?

She forgot her shame, though, when they all sat down in a booth with their tray of food. For a little while she could pretend they were just like any other family in the little restaurant, munching their burgers, talking about what had happened during the day, joking and kidding, and blowing paper wads from their straws at each other.

Later that night it was harder to pretend. First they stopped at the supermarket to pick up a quart of milk and a few apples for the next day. Back in the van, there was no talking. The only sound came from Dad drumming on the steering wheel with his fingers.

"Now where are we going?" asked Hannah brightly.

"Well, let's drive by Sam's station first," suggested Mom. "You'll enjoy meeting him, Harvey."

"Fat chance," muttered Alex.

Old Sam was outside, locking heavy chain-link gates across the front of his station when they drove up. His face wrinkled into a scowl, but he opened the gates for them.

"Well, I see you're back to use the restrooms?"

Mom laughed like he'd said something really funny. "I brought my husband, Harvey, by to meet you, Sam. But since we're here . . ." She motioned to the three kids. "Scoot off to the restrooms to wash up and brush your teeth."

By the time they got back to the van, Dad and Sam were talking like old friends. Dad shook Sam's hand, then started the engine. "It's getting late," he said.

"Hey, wait a minute!" Sam walked around to Mom's window. "Now that you're here and all . . . uh, you got any place to park that minivan tonight?"

"Not exactly," said Mom. "But the Lord will take care of us."

Sam snorted. "I'll tell you what I tell my son when *he's* preachin' at me. The Lord never did nothin' for me. Everything I got, I earned with these two hands." He held up his gnarled, grease-stained hands. "Anyway, drive that rig behind my station." He motioned for Dad to follow as he hobbled stiffly around the corner.

Dad grinned and slowly guided the van after Sam.

"Park right here!" ordered Sam, pointing to an empty space between stacks of used tires and old car parts. "It ain't fancy, but it's safe once I lock these gates. I got my own apartment above the station there."

"Sam, that's the best offer we've had in a long time," said Dad. "We'll be honored to accept it."

Sam grunted and turned to go back inside. "Oh, yeah . . . I got an old two-burner hot plate in the office here in case you want to make some mornin' coffee or heat a can of beans or anything." Without waiting for an answer, he went inside.

"I don't believe this," marveled Katie. "I mean that crabby old man being so nice to us. How come?"

Mom smiled. "I told you Sam appreciated our help this morning. This is his way of saying 'thank you.'"

"It may be that the Lord will give us a chance to help Sam again," said Dad. "Sounds to me like he doesn't know God very well."

Katie wrapped her blanket around herself and snuggled down next to Hannah. "Thanks, God," she whispered. The rest of her prayer dissolved into deep breathing as she fell asleep and slept through the night.

⌒

Their new life in Seattle became a little easier in the days that followed. No one yelled at them or threw things or chased them. Sam told the family that they were welcome to spend nights at his station until they had a better alternative. He even loaned them a rickety folding table where Mom could make Dad's lunches and fix simple breakfasts or suppers. A couple of evenings, they talked Sam into joining them for canned stew or spaghetti.

But while life wasn't quite as tough as it had been, there were still plenty of challenges. Daytimes were the worst—long, hot, and boring. Most mornings after dropping Dad off they went to the small, crowded park. There were no more sightings of Ringo and his gang.

Katie especially hated the long, hot afternoons. There wasn't much to do but wander through the neighborhood stores. Sometimes the clerks would follow behind them like they were a family of scruffy thieves. Mom would quickly march them out the door. "That's the last time we'll be shopping in that store," she'd say through stiff lips.

More and more they would try to find a shady place to

park the van, roll down the windows, and have a nap or read. Alex pored over his tattered comic books while Katie read and reread the one Nancy Drew mystery she had unpacked while they were at Puget Sound Camp.

Dad had to work every single day, even on the weekend. The Washington Grocers Association was anxious to finish the move into their new building. For Katie, the days were beginning to run into each other.

The first day that was different was Wednesday of the following week. When Katie woke that morning and stretched her cramped muscles, she looked out the window at a dark gray sky. "Oh, great," she groaned. "What'll we do all day today if it rains?" But the sky brightened somewhat as the morning went on, and the rain held off. Katie and Hannah were helping Mom make their lunch sandwiches at the park, when the first raindrop hit Katie's nose. Then another. And another. Hurriedly they threw the sandwiches together and bolted into the van to eat.

"Can't we drive somewhere, Mommy?" Hannah begged. She pressed her nose against the window.

Mom started the van. "I don't want to drive very far," she said. "We're running low on gas and lower on money." With the windshield wipers going, she turned out onto a side street. "Let's see where this goes."

Katie was the first one to spot the library, a white frame building with wide cement steps leading to the entry and a row of thick evergreen shrubs on each side. "Wallington Branch of the Seattle Public Library," she read aloud. "Oh, Mom, let's go in. It would be so great to have something new to read."

"I agree." Mom jockeyed the van into the one empty space in the parking lot and stopped. "Hurry in, and be sure to wipe your feet." Everyone dashed across the puddle-filled drive and wet lawn and up the steps.

Inside the warm entryway, they stood on a mat to drip dry and wipe their feet. Then Katie darted ahead.

"Watch out for those ladders and paint cans over along the wall," cautioned Mom. "Someone must be going to paint."

Katie skirted the painting equipment and stepped into the main room. She gave a happy sigh when she saw the hundreds of books shelved in the room. Ignoring the librarian and other library users, she looked around for the teen fiction section. There it was, with three whole shelves of Nancy Drew mysteries.

Picking out one she hadn't read, she went over to an empty reading table and sat down. As she turned to the first page, the library, the other readers, and the rain outside disappeared. Katie was now helping Nancy solve yet another mystery.

A bit later she was surprised to look up and see Mom and Hannah standing beside her. "What's wrong, Mom?"

Mom tapped her watch. "It's time to go pick up your dad from work," she whispered.

"It can't be. We just got here."

Mom smiled. "It's been three hours. Now come on."

Katie looked down at her book. "Mom, can't I stay here and read while you go after Dad? Please?"

Mom looked shocked. "I don't think that's a good idea. Something might—"

"Hey, I'll stay here, too," offered Alex as he joined them. "We'll be fine."

"And we *promise* not to leave the library," coaxed Katie.

"I suppose it'll be all right." Mom still looked worried. "You both be sure to stay right here."

"We will," they answered so loudly that the librarian frowned at them and put her finger to her lips.

After Mom and Hannah left, Alex disappeared. Katie sat back and quickly returned to Nancy Drew and her friend, George.

"Attention, everyone."

Katie dropped her book. "Now what?"

"Please prepare to leave in ten minutes," the librarian's voice crackled out over the intercom. "We will be closing at five this evening so the painters can finish their work. Bring your books to the front desk."

Katie put her book back on the shelf. She started across the room to find Alex. He wasn't in the kid's section. She looked around until she noticed the long double row of computers at the back. Sure enough, there was Alex, hunched over a computer monitor.

Katie grabbed his shoulder. "Come on, Alex, didn't you hear the librarian? The library's closing."

"I can't go yet. I'm trying to e-mail Jeff back in Sunnydale. Just give me a few more minutes."

"No! Everyone's leaving."

Grumbling under his breath, Alex shut down the computer and stood up. "What'll we do now? Mom and Dad won't be back yet."

"I guess we'll have to wait out on the steps." Little pinpoints of fear pricked Katie when she thought of the two of them waiting alone in this strange neighborhood.

With dragging feet, she and Alex followed the last stragglers out the front doors of the library. "At least we can be thankful it's not raining now," she said.

They stood at the railing and watched little kids, teens, and a handful of adults go down the steps one by one, either out to the parking lot or toward the sidewalk. Katie began to feel very alone when they heard the doors being locked behind them and saw the librarian pull mini blinds down over the glass doors. Finally, she and Alex were the only ones still waiting.

Katie looked around and spied a small cluster of shops in the block just below them. "Alex, let's take a walk down the block," she said. "I'm getting tired of people in their cars gawking at us as they drive by."

"We can't leave. We might miss Mom and Dad," protested Alex.

"Suit yourself. I'm going to go. We've got plenty of time." She started down the steps.

"OK, OK." Alex started after her. It didn't take long to walk to the row of shops. Like much of Seattle, the street sloped downhill. But Katie was dismayed to see that most of the stores were empty and boarded up. Only a corner bookshop was brightly lighted.

"I'm going in there," she said.

Alex stood with his feet stubbornly planted on the wet sidewalk. "No way. I'm heading back to the library."

"Well, well, look who's here . . ." said a familiar and frightening voice.

Chapter Ten

*K*atie felt like she had been plunked into a deep freeze. There, in the shadows of the store canopy, stood her trio of enemies from the city park. Their ringleader, Ringo, smiled cruelly, showing his mossy yellow teeth. "Just the girl I've been looking for," he said.

Katie tried to edge past them. "Leave us alone or I'll yell for the police!"

Ringo looked around. "Oh, yeah? I don't see no cops." He grinned over at his tall, dark buddy. "Do you see any cops, Charley?"

Charley smiled widely. "Nope. No cops anywhere."

"So, let's go." Once again, Ringo roughly snatched Katie's arm and twisted it behind her back. He shoved her ahead of him down the street. "Charley, you and Speed bring the curly top." Katie saw Alex's eyes grow dark with anger, but he kept quiet as Charley and the silent Speed flanked him on either side.

Katie stopped. "You can't do anything to us on a downtown street in broad daylight," she said through gritted teeth.

"Wanna bet?" Ringo reached with his free hand into his

baggy pants pocket and drew out a shiny switchblade knife. He flicked it open with his thumb and held the steel blade only inches from Katie's nose. "This is our turf. People know better'n to bother us around here." Alex let out a little squeak of fear and Ringo sneered, then thrust the knife back in his pocket.

When the traffic crossing light turned green, he pushed Katie to cross the street. The others followed. The only remnants of a building on that corner lot was one sagging wall and a crumbling foundation hole. The hole was filled with a neglected tangle of waist-high weeds, dry grass, and vicious blackberry vines.

Katie shivered when the boys shoved her and Alex toward the wall. What were they planning to do with them? *Please, God, help us,* she silently prayed over and over again. What was it Grandma used to say? Something about praying hard like everything depended on God, then working hard like everything depended on you. But what could God expect her to do now? Her free right hand was empty.

Slowly and stealthily, she eased her hand toward her hip pocket and felt her wallet. Maybe Ringo wouldn't know that she didn't have any money in it. "Here!" She held out the wallet. "Let us go, and you can have everything in it."

Ringo laughed, but he looked greedily at the plump wallet. "Like we didn't plan to take all your money anyway," he jeered. "Here, let me see that." For a fraction of a minute he dropped her arm and reached for the wallet.

Katie was ready. Faster than a bolt of summer lightning, she raised her arm and gave the wallet a mighty toss, deep into the gnarled tangle of weeds and berry vines.

"Why, you little . . ." Ringo and Speed dived after it, like a couple of scrawny rats chasing a bread crust. The third guy, Charley, held back long enough to look at Katie and mouth the word, "Go!"

She didn't wait to thank him. Snatching Alex's hand, she yanked him toward the street.

There was a screech of brakes as a long oil delivery truck managed to stop for them. Katie could feel her heart thumping almost as loudly as her footsteps until they made the crossing safely. Now the oil truck and several cars blocked the street crossing. She could hear Ringo screaming and cursing at them across the street.

Alex jerked his hand free, and they hurried toward the lighted bookstore. The lights dimmed just as they approached the door. A young African-American woman with a stylish Afro hairdo came out carrying a leather briefcase. She stopped to lock the door, then looked up at Katie and smiled pleasantly. "Sorry, we're closed now."

"Oh, please let us inside!" begged Katie. "Those three creeps across the street are after me and my brother."

The woman glanced across the street and frowned. Turning, she unlocked the door. She pushed Katie and Alex inside, followed them in, and speedily locked the door. "We've tolerated those three bullies in this neighborhood long enough," she said. "They'll do any horrible thing to get money for their next drug fix. Druggies!" She hissed the word.

"You know them?" asked Katie.

The woman's face twisted into a sour smile. "The tall black creep is my nephew Charles. Believe it or not, he was a pretty decent kid until he took up with that Ringo." By now there was a loud pounding of feet as the evil trio dashed up to the door. Quickly, the woman pulled a cellular phone from her briefcase and dialed 9-1-1. "This is Liz Barton, from Barton's Books," she said loudly. "I wish to make a complaint." Katie thankfully watched the trio slink away down the street.

When her call was completed, Liz Barton turned to Alex and Katie. "The police say they'll be here as soon as possible. Unfortunately, with so many complaints, they're always short-handed. Those bullies will be long gone by the time the officers get here."

Katie stared at her. "You called the police on your own nephew?"

The bookstore owner looked near tears. "Getting stopped by the police may be the one thing that can save Charles."

"He's not all bad," said Katie helpfully. "He had the chance to keep us from getting away, and he let us go. Don't give up on Charles yet."

Alex pulled at her arm. "We gotta go back to the library right away. Mom and Dad'll be waiting."

"Is there a back door?" asked Katie nervously. Liz Barton motioned for them to follow her to the rear of the store, where she unlocked a door leading to the alleyway. "Go up to the next traffic light," she said. "Then walk two blocks straight up the hill to the library. Good luck, kids. I'll be praying for you."

"And we'll be praying for your nephew. Thanks a lot," replied Katie. Liz was still watching them as they crept along the cluttered alleyway to the street corner. No one was in sight.

"Let's go!" Katie hissed when the traffic light turned green.

She and Alex ran across the street and pelted up the sidewalk, making no sound except for their raspy breathing and their thudding feet.

Alex collapsed in a heavy heap on the bottom step of the library stairs. Sweat streamed off his red face.

Katie climbed up to the top step and began pounding on the locked door. No one came. All she could hear was the loud booming beat of rock music. Twisting her head to peer through a gap in the blinds, she spied a giant boom box sitting on the hall table. Beyond were the painters, laughing and talking while they slapped paint on the library walls.

Katie sadly realized they would never hear her. She turned and went back down to Alex.

"Mom and Dad aren't here yet," he said glumly.

"I know. I can't make the painters hear me, either. We've got to get out of sight." She looked about the yard and spied a thick row of evergreen shrubs on either side of the cement stairs. "Come on."

Wearily, Alex dragged himself to his feet and followed her. They managed to push the prickly bushes apart wide enough to crawl behind them into the space next to the building. Katie brushed a mass of dusty cobwebs from her face. "We can still see Mom and Dad when they come," she said softly. "But I don't think anyone will spot us here."

Alex plopped down heavily on the dry ground. The earlier rain hadn't even touched this protected spot. "Katie, what'll we do if Mom and Dad don't come back?" His shoulders were hunched over and his head drooped.

"Well, of course they'll come. They wouldn't leave us here

alone, silly." Even as she reassured him, Katie silently asked herself the same question. Where were Mom and Dad? They should have been back long before now. It was hard to swallow, because her throat was so dry. She wiped her sweaty palms on the grungy, stained legs of her jeans. Maybe there had been an accident or something.

"Listen, what's that?" Alex lifted his head and strained to look out. "I see someone climbing up the steps."

"Shhh!" Katie pushed back a branch. She spied a pair of long legs in faded blue denims. Holding her breath, she pried the branches further apart. "Dad!" Ignoring the scratches, she and Alex shoved their way around the hedge and ran to the safety of Dad's open arms.

Katie heard the car doors slamming in the parking lot. Mom and Hannah came hurrying up to them. "Alex? Katie? Are you all right?" asked Mom. "Why weren't you waiting inside?"

"We had to leave the library, Mom." Katie stood there pulling cobwebs and twigs from her short hair. "The library closed at five this evening so the men could finish painting."

"We waited and waited and you didn't come," accused Alex.

"Oh, kids, I'm so sorry." Mom's face had turned white. "The van ran out of gas on the way back here. I knew the tank was low, but we were out of money." She put an arm around both of them. "Did you poor kids hide behind those bushes the whole time?"

"No." Katie hung her head guiltily. "When you and Dad didn't show up, I talked Alex into taking a little walk down where those shops are." She had to take a deep breath before she could go on. "Then—then we met those three awful boys from the park. They forced us to go with them to a vacant lot."

Dad flinched like someone had hit him in the face. "And?"

"They had a switchblade," Alex said, picking up the story. "Mom, those guys were real creeps. But Katie fixed 'em." He looked over at his sister and grinned proudly. "She offered 'em everything in her billfold. Then she pitched it in some berry vines. When the creeps went after it, we got away." He looked anxiously at Katie. "Hey, I hope you didn't really have much money in there."

Katie smiled. "The only things in that wallet were two folded sheets of paper in case I decided to write a letter." She scratched her head. "But, Dad, how did you and Mom get the van back here if you ran out of gas and didn't have money?"

Dad patted his back hip pocket. "Oh, we've got money now. The boss surprised us and gave us our checks today. Your mom and Hannah and I had to walk around the streets until we found a bank to cash my check. Then we picked up a five-gallon can of gas. We'll fill the tank at Sam's tonight."

Katie leaned forward. "You got paid, though, so that means we can quit living on the streets, doesn't it?" She didn't even feel tired anymore.

Dad held up his hand. "Not so fast, hon. My news isn't all good. We got paid because the warehouse work ended today."

"But not for you, right Dad?" asked Alex. "They're keeping you on, aren't they?"

"Nope. Sorry, son." Dad lifted a tired and dirty-faced Hannah up to perch on his shoulder and started toward the van. "It looks like that promise of a steady job was just a come-on to keep us working until the move was finished."

"Dad, are you saying we're going to keep on living like this?" Katie's voice cracked.

Dad shook his head. "No, Katie, I'm not. Certainly not after what happened to you kids this afternoon. The question is, just where can we go next?"

An idea clicked in Katie's head. "How about that campground called Seamist?" she suggested hopefully.

"That would be nice," agreed Mom. "Problem is, those state campgrounds charge fifteen dollars a night. Dad's pay won't last long at that rate."

"Then where . . ."

Dad gently sat Hannah in the van and motioned for the rest of them to follow. Clicking on his seat belt, he started the engine and backed away from the library. "It seems to me it's about time for us to head up to Crooked Bend," he said as he shifted gears.

"Crooked Bend? Hey, that sounds like an Old West town for outlaws," said Alex.

Dad chuckled. "Nothing like that. It's a campground up in the foothills above some town called Mapleton. A fellow at work told me about it. Pretty primitive, but there's no camping fees."

"Crooked Bend, here we come!" Alex shouted.

"Even a tent home up in the hills sounds pretty good to me right now," said Mom.

Katie didn't speak. Sure, anything was better than staying on these streets, but they were still a family of gypsies. It was almost the first of August. She was becoming afraid. Not only would they not be going back to Sunnydale by the time school started, at this rate they wouldn't even have a place to live in Washington.

"Let's hurry," said Hannah, bouncing up and down in her seat. "We can surprise Sam and tell him we're leaving tomorrow."

But Sam had a few surprises himself that evening.

Chapter Eleven

*D*arkness was dropping over Seattle when the Barnes family reached Sam's service station. Dad drove right up to the gas pump and stopped.

"What's that big sign say?" Hannah pointed to a bright yellow sign with black lettering out by the street.

Katie twisted around to look. "Business for sale," she read out loud. "Hey, everyone, Sam must be selling his station!"

Just then Sam walked up to Dad's window. "Now, don't tell me you folks are actually gonna buy something?"

Dad's deep laugh rang out. "Fill 'er up. Say, what's up with that sign over there? Are you selling out, Sam?"

Sam's scowl got blacker. "Yeah, it's all that environmental stuff. The bigwigs are tellin' me my underground tanks ain't safe. I can't afford to replace 'em, so I'm pullin' out. I'm afraid you'll have to find some other place to stay after next week."

"That's no problem," said Mom. "We're moving on to-morrow anyway. But where will *you* go, Sam?"

"He'll be moving down to Bend, Oregon," said a strange voice. Katie saw a man about Dad's age coming from the office, a friendly smile on his face. He looked a lot like Sam, if Sam were a lot younger and ever looked pleasant.

"Why, you must be Sam's son," said Mom.

The man's smile grew wider. "That's right. My mom used to call me 'Little Sam.' You folks must be the Barnes family. I've been hearing about you." He glanced over at his dad, who was pumping gas into the thirsty van. "My family and I have been trying for years to get Dad to leave this old station and move down by us." He sighed. "Dad's been kind of bitter about God and Christians ever since Mom died twelve years ago. Then when his only child became a pastor . . ." He shook his head.

By now everyone was out of the van and crowding around this friendly man. "So how'd you change his mind?" asked Katie.

Young Sam's smile came back. "I didn't. You folks did. A couple of days ago I called Pop and he said he'd found out it wasn't too bad living near a family of Christians. I drove up here this morning, and now he's going to go back with me." He put his arm around Alex's shoulder and smiled at each of them. "Thanks, folks, for being nice to my ornery old pop. And praise the Lord for bringing you here."

"Amen," said Dad, walking over to join them. "Sam's been very kind to us, too—he gave us a place to stay nights. It's good to see how God takes care of his children, isn't it?" Dad's smile matched young Sam's. "Hey, I've got an idea. There's a real good little hamburger place over on the next street. We'd be honored if you two would be our guests for cheeseburgers tonight."

⌐

Early Friday afternoon, the van rumbled merrily down the I-5 freeway. Its gas tank was full of Sam's very best gas, and there were three new bags of groceries crammed in the back.

Alex hung over Katie's seat, yakking in her ear. "I hope we get to stop for cheeseburgers again tonight. Don't you, Katie?"

Katie leaned away from him. "You ate enough of them last night to last a week, Alex."

"Hey, it was fun. A lot better'n being chased by thugs downtown! Admit it—after the crummy afternoon you and I had, last night was pretty decent."

Katie agreed with him. "Young Sam's cool, isn't he?" she added. "A lot better than that stuck-up Reverend Lawrence who chased us off last week."

Alex grinned. "Young Sam tells great jokes, too. Even Old Sam laughed."

Katie smiled, remembering how much she herself had laughed last night. She hadn't done much smiling this summer.

Things could be a lot worse, she knew. At least her family was still together. Not to mention the fact that they'd seen the last of Ringo and his buddies back in Seattle. And Old Sam was going to be looked after. She knew that meant a lot to Mom and Dad.

Katie closed her eyes and leaned back against the seat, but a little imp of doubt bounced around in her head. "Our lives are as bad off as ever," argued the imp. "Here we are, driving down the freeway again. No job. No home. Nothing but the rumor of some free campground. It's already early August. School starts soon. Problems, problems, problems. . . ."

"Next stop, Crooked Bend!" Dad's voice jolted Katie awake. Groggily, she shook her sleepy head and peeked out the window. The terrain looked little like Seattle here. No shops and few houses. Soon she saw mostly trees and green growth. The sleek freeway lay behind them, and the van was bouncing up a steep graveled road. Hannah jostled against Katie when a tire hit a pothole.

"Hey, look—no railings!" A wide-awake Alex stared out his window. "Hope we don't go over the side. Ha, ha! This Crooked Bend's not for sissies, is it, Dad."

Dad laughed. "No, but I figure we'll manage just fine." He steered the van right. They bounced down a narrow winding road into an open, tree-dotted campground. A weathered sign on a leaning post read, "Crooked Bend."

"Here we are," said Dad. He braked the van to a stop.

Groaning and stretching stiff muscles, they all unbuckled and climbed out. Mom looked all about her, then raised her head and inhaled deeply. "Oh my, I'd forgotten how good the woods smell."

"It's sure quiet," said Katie. "Are we the only campers here?"

Dad sniffed the air. "No. I smell a campfire. Someone's not far away." He reached into the back seat and lifted a drowsy Hannah out in his arms. Alex clambered after them.

"Howdy, folks!" said a squeaky voice. They spun around to see a tiny figure trotting across the roadway. The man wasn't much taller than Katie, and so skinny that he looked like a stiff breeze might blow him away. When he pulled off his blue stocking cap, his bald head glistened in the afternoon sunlight. "Looking for a place to camp?" he asked.

"We hope to," replied Dad. "Are you in charge here, sir?"

"Yep. Shorty Jackson's my name. I'm kind of the unofficial caretaker." Shorty waited while Dad introduced his family, then waved his arm toward several empty campsites. "Take your choice. Folks have snatched up the others back in the trees."

"I don't *see* anyone else," complained Katie. "Where is everybody?"

"Most of the folks who come up to Crooked Bend like their privacy," explained Shorty. "You likely won't see much of them except at the water pump around the bend there or at one of the two outhouses." He pointed at two small buildings over to the right. He smiled at Mom. "Are you familiar with outhouses, ma'am?"

Mom's serious face broke into a smile. "I've lived all my life on farms in Kansas," she replied. "I know all about outhouses and hand-operated water pumps."

"Good." Shorty nodded his bald head. "Then I'll leave you folks to pick out your site and get settled. There's plenty of dead wood around for your campfire." He turned and walked briskly back to a small, older trailer house half-hidden in the tall trees.

In less than twenty minutes they had selected a campsite, one with two young maple trees that Mom figured would be good clothesline posts. Soon the rolled-up tent and stakes were unloaded. While Mom and Alex tied up the clothesline rope between the trees, Katie helped Dad set up the tent once again.

"Seems like old times, doesn't it, Dad?" she asked as she pounded a tent stake into the rocky soil.

Dad poked his head out of the jumble of canvas and tent stakes. "Sure does, honey. We've set this old tent up plenty of times this summer, haven't we? The good Lord willing, this'll be the last. We should be settled in our own place by fall."

"Uh-huh," said Katie. Dad sounded so hopeful, she didn't want to confess her fears and doubts. She sure didn't want to mention the missing money from Grandma. Maybe Dad was right; maybe she *was* worrying for nothing. This truly was a beautiful and peaceful place.

For their first evening at Crooked Bend, Mom fixed the family's favorite camp meal. On little squares of aluminum foil she placed a hamburger patty, then added cut-up potatoes, carrots, and onions. She cooked the packets on the fireplace coals. "We'd better enjoy this fresh meat and milk tonight," she said. "By tomorrow the ice we bought will all be melted."

The food tasted so yummy after all those days of cold sandwiches and canned spaghetti, that Katie surprised herself by volunteering to wash the supper dishes. Even more amazing, Alex offered to dry.

"Let's go for a walk through the campground when we finish, Katie," he suggested. "Maybe we can spot some of the other campers."

"OK." Katie wrung out the soapy dishrag. "I got a glimpse of two girls pumping water, but by the time I got down there, they'd disappeared."

"Makes you wonder, doesn't it?" said Alex suspiciously.

By the time the last dish was dried and they started down

the road, their evening walk had turned into a nighttime stroll. They rounded the big bend in the narrow road and passed the old-fashioned water pump. They could smell smoking campfires and frying food. From a distant group of evergreen trees shone the soft light of a camp lantern. Katie heard the clean whack of an axe splitting a chunk of wood, a barking dog, and the hushed voices of people talking and laughing. But no one came out where they could see them.

Suddenly, they heard *creak-creak, creak-creak*, and the sound of water splashing into a container.

"Someone's gettin' water at the pump," Alex whispered.

Katie turned to peer down the road. She strained her eyes to see in the dusk. Then she gasped and yanked at Alex's arm. "Do you see that man down at the pump?"

Alex snickered. "Yeah, he has to use two hands to work the pump handle."

"Alex, I think that guy's Mr. Van Switt! You know, Gwen Van Switt's dad back at Puget Sound Park?"

"Gwen Van Switt? Are you talkin' about that snobby girl who you say stole Grandma's chest? That's crazy, Katie. What would rich people like them be doing in a place like Crooked Bend?"

"I don't know, but it looks like him!" said Katie fiercely. "If he's here, so is Gwen. And if she still has that chest, I'm going to get it back!" Katie started toward the pump. "Mr. Van Switt, is that you?" she called. "Please, wait a minute." In the graying darkness she saw the man straighten up, look toward her, then snatch up his water bucket. For just a moment, she had a good look at his face.

"Mr. Van Switt, I'm Katie Barnes!" she shouted. "I met your daughter, Gwen, back at Puget Sound Campground. I even ate lunch with her one Sunday. Don't you remember?"

"Never saw you before in my life," snarled a raspy voice. He began coughing, a loose, phlegmy cough. "Smoker's cough," Gwen had called it.

"Come on, Katie," pleaded Alex. "Let's go."

"No!" Katie raced after the shadowy figure. "Please, Mr. Van Switt, this is important! I've got to talk to Gwen."

The man stopped. "Now listen, Miss—whatever your name is. I don't know you, and for your information, I'm traveling alone. No daughter. Quit bothering me!" Katie could only hear his fading footsteps.

"Someday, Katie," hissed Alex, "you're gonna stick that nose in the wrong place once too often, and then you'll be sorry. I'm going back to our camp."

Katie stood there feeling torn apart. More than anything she wanted to follow Mr. Van Switt. Still, it was nearly dark outside. Reluctantly, she turned to follow after her brother. "The minute the sun comes up tomorrow morning," she vowed to herself, "I'm gonna search every inch of this campground until I can pound on the door of that big fancy motor home."

Her mother was waiting, hands on her hips, when Katie walked into camp. "Katie Barnes, Alex tells me that not only were you talking to a strange man, you were arguing with him. How many times—"

"Whoa, Mom." Katie held out her hand to ward off the sharp words. "That man was Mr. Van Switt, Gwen's dad. This means Gwen's here at Crooked Bend, and I have a chance to get Grandma's little chest back from her."

"The Van Switts camping here? That doesn't seem likely."

"It was him, Mom. Even though it was getting dark, I recognized him. The minute I heard his smoker's hack, I knew for sure. I'm going to find them tomorrow morning."

"We'll talk about that tomorrow, Katie." Mom's stern voice ended the conversation, but *not* Katie's determination.

Chapter Twelve

"Go to sleep, huh?" Katie muttered to herself as she turned and tossed in her sleeping bag. How could Mom expect her to sleep after she had spotted Mr. Van Switt down by the pump? Did the family even believe her? Well, it didn't matter. Katie knew what she had seen and heard. For some reason the Van Switts were up here at Crooked Bend. "I'll find them in the morning," she vowed.

Over and over she plotted how she would scout the campground until she spied that giant blue and silver motor home. She knotted her fists and imagined pounding on the door. When Gwen answered, Katie would demand that she return the little chest she'd stolen.

Whew, it was sure stuffy in the tent. Alex had the right idea; he had dragged his sleeping bag outside to sleep. When Hannah started coughing, then jabbed Katie with her bony little knee, Katie sat up. She quietly gathered her bag, unzipped the tent fly, and crawled outside with the sleeping bag in tow. Blindly, she felt her way over the rough ground until she touched a big, soft mound near the table.

"Pssst, Alex!" She jostled him with her foot.

"Ooph!" he grunted. His fuzzy head reared up. "Katie, what are you doing out here in the middle of the night?"

"Shhh! It was too hot." Katie plopped her bag onto the ground and sat on it. "Alex, I can't sleep. When I get Grandma's chest back in the morning, I just know everything's going to go better for us."

"Not likely," scoffed her brother. "Even if by some weird chance that *was* Gwen's dad and you really get the chest back, so what? It ain't magic."

"You just don't know." Katie felt tempted to tell him what was hidden in the secret drawer of the chest. *I don't dare,* she thought. *Not until I hold the money in my hand . . . which should be soon.*

"Listen!" said Alex's voice from the darkness. "I hear a car coming through the campground!"

Katie held her breath. The roar of a motor drew closer. Suddenly two huge headlights blinded them, momentarily brightening their surroundings. A long, square shape with dim lights at each corner rumbled down the roadway past their camp, turned toward the main road, and disappeared. Katie felt her heart thud. "Alex, did you see the color of that motor home?"

"Blue and silver. I'm pretty sure it had California plates, too. Looks like maybe you were right after all." He lay down and turned his back to her. "But a lot of good your great detective work did. . . ." Within minutes he was breathing evenly.

Katie shivered and climbed into her bag. Trying not to cry, she stared up at the bit of sky that showed through the tall, ragged tree limbs. The faraway stars looked cold and unfriendly. She tried to swallow the giant lump in her throat, but it just seemed to get bigger and bigger. The sky was turning gray when she finally felt her eyelids grow heavy.

The next thing Katie was aware of was the pungent smell of campfire smoke. She rubbed her eyes, which were stinging from the smoke, and struggled into a sitting position. "Dad, why are you starting the fire so early?"

Dad was bent over the small stone fireplace, fanning the flame with his cap. "Early, nothing. Rise and shine, kids! It's nearly eight o'clock."

Alex moaned and scrunched further down in his bag. Mom walked up and set a heavy kettle of water on the fireplace grill. "It really is time to get up, kids," she urged. "This is going to be a busy day."

"Not for me," Katie said bitterly. Then she told her parents about the Van Switts' sneaky getaway. They didn't look sympathetic.

"I hope you realize now that even if you did see Mr. Van Switt last night, it's time for you to forget about the chest," said Mom angrily. "Anyway, you've been accusing Gwen of stealing from you without any proof. Just let it go, Katie."

"You know Grandma Ross will understand," Dad said, adding another piece of wood to the smoldering fire.

Alex loudly yawned and stretched, then asked, "What did you mean about this being such a busy day, Mom?"

The intense look on Mom's face softened to a smile. "This is Sunday. Tonight we're going to have a church service and invite our neighbors."

"Mom!" Katie had started toward the tent, but now she stood frozen. "We haven't even *met* any of these people. Couldn't we just have a private Bible study?"

"No," said Mom firmly. "The Bible tells Christians not to forsake the gathering of themselves together. And we're not going to disappoint God."

"So how do we know any of these campers are Christians?" demanded Katie. "They sure haven't been friendly."

"Yeah." For once Alex was in agreement with her. "The way they're hidin' away, they're probably robbers or killers running from the police."

"I think you'll be surprised," said Dad. He turned from the fire that was finally burning brightly. "I know Shorty Jackson is no robber or killer, and he thinks this is a great idea. Matter of fact, he's offered to play his harmonica for the songs we'll be singing."

"Songs?" Once again Katie felt despair. "But, Dad, you know none of us can sing. Who'll lead the singing?"

Dad's grin deepened the small crinkles around his eyes. "I may not be much of a singer," he said, "but I can sure make a joyful noise unto the Lord, as the Good Book commands." He picked up his hatchet and a chunk of wood. "There is power, power, wonder-working power," he sang loudly and tunelessly, chopping kindling in time with the notes.

Katie closed her eyes. It was happening again. Just when she thought things couldn't get any worse, they did. Behind her closed eyelids, she pictured that little bald-headed gnome, Shorty Jackson, blowing away on his harmonica while her tone-deaf dad led the song service. She wished she could put Sunday on hold so evening would never come.

She couldn't. Sunday whizzed by like one of the huge Boeing jets that soared across the sky. After morning cleanup, Mom and Dad went up the roadway seeking out their new neighbors. Katie and Alex struggled to pull logs around the fireplace to make room for more people to sit. Hannah picked a raggedy bouquet of weeds and ferns and set them in a jar on the table.

The service was set for seven o'clock. Shorty Jackson was there by six-thirty. He polished his harmonica on the long sleeve of his flannel shirt. "How about, 'Work, for the Night Is Coming,'" he suggested.

"Great!" Dad jotted down the title on a scrap of brown paper bag. "Do you know 'Blessed Assurance'?" The two of them bent their heads over the paper. Katie and Alex, with a wriggling Hannah between them, perched on a log near the fireplace.

"No one'll come tonight," said Alex.

"We should be so lucky," scoffed Katie. "Look!" She pointed to an old man and woman making their way toward them. The woman struggled with a walker. Behind them strolled a bearded man who held the hand of a small boy, trailed by a spotted hound dog. "Folks'll come," continued Katie. "I just hope they don't turn around and leave again when they hear the music." She could hear soft voices and shuffling feet as people sat on the rough log benches.

Finally, Dad looked at his watch and stood up. "Well, friends, I know you're all here to praise the Lord. Shorty and I figured we'd start out by singing an old favorite. Shorty, why don't you play a few bars first?" Dad's grin gleamed white in the firelight. "I know everyone will recognize this song right away."

Shorty's mouth moved back and forth across the harmonica, making some amazing sounds.

"What in the world is he playing?" asked Katie quietly.

Alex shrugged. "Don't ask me. I'm as tone-deaf as Dad."

Suddenly, a slight, dark-haired man with a guitar tucked under his arm strode from the back. He walked up to join Dad and Shorty. Two teenage girls, their heads shyly tucked down, followed him. "I'm Felipe Gomez," the man said. "Mind if we join you folks with your music?"

"Well, praise the Lord!" shouted Dad. "He sent us some more musicians. All right, everybody. Let's sing 'Work, for the Night Is Coming.'"

As the rich chords of the guitar and the voices of the newcomers rang out, other voices shakily joined in. Katie marveled. It sounded like the singing was going straight up through the tall trees to the starry sky and maybe to the very throne of God himself. Still, she couldn't help asking a question of God. Since it was now pretty clear God was at work in Washington, too, why didn't he help the Barnes family get back on track this summer? Surely God remembered that school would start in less than a month. "I'm not trying to second-guess you, Lord," she whispered under the sound of the music. "I just wish I could talk with You, person to person."

When the song service ended, several people shared favorite Bible verses or talked about blessings from God. After a closing prayer, everyone began to leave as quietly as they had come. Each stopped to thank Mom and Dad for inviting them.

Katie hurried to catch the younger of the two girl singers, who looked to be about her own age. "I'm Katie Barnes," she said. "Thanks a lot for helping my dad with the singing tonight. I'm afraid we Barneses aren't very good singers. You were great."

"I'm Maria Gomez." The girl brushed her shoulder-length black hair from her face and smiled timidly. "I guess we're pretty good singers because we sing so much. We go into Seattle and perform every week."

"Wow! You mean you're professional singers?" Katie was impressed. "Where do you sing?"

"Oh, every Friday our family and Uncle Pete's family go into Seattle and sing at the Pike Place Market. Afterward, Uncle Pete passes the hat around and, usually, we do really well."

Katie stared at her new friend. "You mean you beg for money after you sing?"

Maria's pretty face turned red in the firelight. "It's not begging," she snapped. "We practice hard and put on a real good program. We have lots of Texas folk songs and some good old country church hymns." She turned to leave.

"Hey, I'm sorry," said Katie. "I didn't mean to make you feel bad. I think it's neat that your family can all sing together." She put her hand on Maria's tan arm. "I sure hope we can be friends. Please."

Maria's smile came back. "Me, too. Listen, my folks are waiting now, but why don't you come to our camp tomorrow? It's the third place after the water pump." Turning, she disappeared into the inky blackness.

After Shorty Jackson had gone, Mom sat the family down to a late supper of corn flakes and milk. Within minutes, small Hannah's head was drooping sleepily over her bowl.

Mom laughed. "I think this family could use a good night's

sleep. It's been a wonderful evening, but I can hardly keep my eyes open." She yawned wearily.

"Just look at those stars in the sky!" exclaimed Dad. "I don't think I've ever felt closer to God than tonight." He picked up a drowsy Hannah and started toward the tent. Hannah coughed and gave a sleepy little cry.

Soon Katie and Alex were snuggled down in their sleeping bags. They were too tired to lug their bags outdoors. The last sound Katie heard before she fell asleep was the baying of the little hound at his campsite.

⌒

The first morning sound Katie heard was Mom's voice yelling, "Oh, no! Look what's happened to all our food!"

Bounding up from her sleeping bag, Katie fumbled until she found her shoes and blue jeans. As she yanked on her clothes, she saw daylight through the tent opening. "Mom, what's wrong?" She stepped outside and into a mud puddle. "Yuk!" The early morning sky was dark gray, and a chilly wind was blowing bits of paper and trash around camp.

Mom was standing over by the table, holding a dripping loaf of bread. "It rained last night. We were all so tired, we forgot to put the boxes of food away in the van." Still wearing her nightgown and with her feet bare, Mom sat down on a wet bench. "Everything's ruined," she moaned. "Bread, pancake flour, crackers, oatmeal, corn flakes—everything but our canned food is worthless!"

"What'll we do?" Katie stepped over to the fireplace to warm herself, only to find it cold and dead. Where was Dad?

Why hadn't he started the fire? She looked around, then caught her breath. "Mom, the van's not here! Dad must be gone. Do you suppose he went to buy more food?"

"Your dad's gone?" Mom scanned the camp as if she hoped he was hiding behind a tree. "But we *can't* buy more food. We only have enough money left to keep the van in gas." Mom's hands were tightly clasped in her lap. Tears dripped down her drawn cheeks.

Katie was scared—more scared than she'd been all summer. Why hadn't Dad told them he was leaving? "Mom, what'll we do without Dad?"

Chapter Thirteen

*M*om didn't say anything at first. She just sat there on the bench in her nightgown, staring at her hands. Then she stood up straight and looked Katie square in the eye. "What will we do?" she asked. "Why, we'll do what we do every morning. We'll build a fire and fix some breakfast and clean up this place before your dad gets back."

She started sorting through the soggy food until she picked up a can of baked beans. "Alex can start the fire while I dress, and then I'll heat the beans. Katie, you go get a bucket of water for dishes."

Soon Katie could hear Alex grumbling as Mom rousted him from his sleeping bag. His grumbling became howls when Mom told him that, since the kindling was wet, they'd need to use a couple of his precious comic books to help start the fire.

Katie smiled to herself and walked up the road to the water pump. It was good to have Mom being more like her normal take-charge self again.

Alex's campfire smoked and smoldered for nearly an hour before it began to put out heat. Soon, though, the bubbling pan of beans smelled so good that their stomachs began to rumble.

Hannah sat at the table, huddled in a blanket. "I never had beans for breakfast before," she complained.

"Well, it's a whole lot better'n oatmeal," Alex said, jamming a heaping forkful into his mouth and reaching for the pan again.

"No!" Katie snatched it back. "That's for Dad."

"Yeah? And what if Dad doesn't come back?" jeered Alex. "What if he just keeps going?"

Mom took the pan and scraped the last few beans onto Alex's plate. "Here, you'd better finish these so you'll have strength for all the extra chores I'm lining up for you today. Don't worry, Katie. The minute your dad gets back, I'll fix him something to eat."

Even with the chores, the morning crawled by slower than a snail inching along a tree branch. Heads kept turning toward the road, listening for the brown minivan.

"Howdy, everybody." Shorty Jackson's cheery face was a welcome sight. "Say, did you have any trouble in that rainstorm last night?"

"Our food got all wet," said Hannah, her eyes big and sad like a cocker spaniel's. "And Daddy's gone, and Mommy doesn't know where he is, and—"

"Shhh!" Katie nudged her. "That's enough, Hannah!"

Shorty reached down and patted Hannah's curls. "I'm sure sorry about that, honey." He turned and headed back to his trailer.

Minutes later he returned carrying a loaf of bread, which he handed to Mom. "I thought maybe you folks could use this."

"Oh, no. You keep it for yourself, Shorty," said Mom. "We'll be fine as soon as Harvey gets back."

"I know you will," said Shorty. "But it's gettin' near lunch-time, and you got three growing kids. Besides," he grinned, "a loaf of bread wouldn't begin to repay the joy I got from coming to your service last night. That was a real 'praise the Lord' meeting."

They all turned to watch as an old rusty pickup and an equally ancient car passed through the campground.

The vehicles' horns blasted and the people inside waved at them. "Bye, Katie!" a girl's voice shouted.

"It's Maria!" Katie enthusiastically waved back. "They must be going shopping."

Shorty shook his head. "Nope, the Gomez family'll be working their way back to Texas." He raised both hands to wave. "God go with you!" he shouted after them.

"You mean they're gone for good?" Katie felt a lump in her throat. "I didn't even get to go visit Maria."

"Well, the family's been up here in the camp a couple of weeks, working on that old car," explained Shorty. "I reckon they're anxious to get to Texas before school starts."

Katie jammed her hands in the pockets of her jeans and turned away. *Nothing lasts when you live like gypsies,* she thought.

After Shorty left to check on other camping families, Mom made up some sandwiches. No one was very hungry. Even Alex could only eat one double sandwich. Hannah wrapped hers to save for her daddy. Her face was flushed, and she soon went into the tent to take a nap.

"The poor girl's getting bronchitis again," Mom said. "I

can tell by that cough." She got out a couple of Dad's old blue work shirts and her sewing box. "I'd better get your dad's work clothes mended," she said to Katie and Alex. "When he gets a job, he won't have any clothes fit to wear." She sat down at the table. "Why don't you read to me from the Bible while I sew, Katie."

Not very excited by the idea, Katie shrugged her shoulders. "What'll I read?"

Her mom pushed the Bible across the table toward her. "How about the eleventh chapter of Hebrews?"

"The whole thing?" Katie sighed deeply, thumbed through the Bible, and found the place. "'Now faith is being sure of what we hope for and certain of what we do not see,'" she read out loud. She stopped and looked up. "This is one of those lessons from the Bible for *me*, isn't it?"

Mom squinted as she held a needle up and threaded it. "No, hon, this is for me today. When I hear you reading about all those folks in the Bible who had trials and tribulations and still kept their faith in God, it gives me a boost, too. Keep reading."

By this time Alex had dropped the ragged comic book he was reading and had joined them around the table. It seemed to Katie that every hero in the whole Bible was mentioned in that eleventh chapter of Hebrews. "'By faith the walls of Jericho fell down,'" she read.

"Listen!" Alex held up his hand and turned toward the road.

Holding her breath, Katie listened with all her might. Could it be? Yes! A car engine was chug-chugging up the hill. When the familiar dusty brown van turned into Crooked

Bend, she let out her breath in a big, whooshy sigh of relief. "It's Dad!"

"I knew you'd be back, Dad!" Alex leaped up and ran to the van. Mom and Katie just looked at each other and rolled their eyes.

"Daddy?" A sleepy-eyed Hannah crept from the tent to join them as Dad stepped from the van.

"Sorry I took so long, everybody." Dad flashed his big grin and set a large box of groceries on the table.

"We thought you were gone for good, Daddy," said Hannah with a quiver in her voice.

Dad's grin faded. He looked quickly over at Mom. "Didn't you read my note? I hung it on the nail right by the tent." He strode up to the tall fir tree. Someone had pounded a rusty nail into the trunk. A tiny scrap of paper still clung to the nail. It flicked back and forth in the chilly breeze.

Katie walked over and picked off the scrap of paper. "It looks like this is all that's left of your note, Dad. The wind probably blew it clear across the campground."

Mom had been sitting silently at the table. Tears streamed down her face. "We don't need the note." Her voice trembled. "We've got your dad right here." The whole family rushed up to Dad and gave him a group hug.

"So where *did* you go, Dad?" asked Alex.

Dad sat down on a bench and let an eager Hannah perch on his knee. "First, I just planned to drive to that little service station a few miles down the hill." He sighed. "When I got there, the station was still closed. Then I remembered one of the fellows at the service last night telling me about a food bank in one of the towns down in the valley."

"A food bank!" Mom stood up with her hands on her hips. "Do you mean to tell me we're begging for food now, Harvey?"

"No, Sarah," soothed Dad. "I worked all day building new shelves at that food bank to pay for the food. That's why I'm so late. Anyway, the food bank was where I met Joe." Dad looked back toward the van just as a white station wagon pulled up. "Who in the world—" began Mom.

"Shhh. This is a new friend I want you all to meet."

The door of the station wagon swung open. A young man with brown hair down to his shoulders, a short pointed beard, and wire-rimmed glasses jumped out. He was carrying a bulky camera and what looked like a tape recorder.

Dad beamed and held out a hand to him. "This young fellow is Joe Jeffers," he said. "We met at the food bank." Dad turned toward Mom. "Joe's a newspaper reporter. He's doing an article about homeless folks, and he wants to take a few pictures."

"Harvey, do you want everyone to know we're penniless?" asked Mom in obvious disbelief.

"It won't do any harm, Sarah, and it might do some good. Maybe someone who has jobs available will read the article and see our pictures."

"No one's gonna print *my* picture in any newspaper," shouted Katie. She dashed into the tent, jerked down the flap, and threw herself on her sleeping bag.

All she could hear was the dim rumble of voices. There was Dad's deep voice, a higher pitched one that must be the reporter, and now and then a word or two from Mom. Finally, curiosity got the better of her. She crawled over to the tent flap and stuck her nose and one eye up to the crack so she could listen and look.

The snoopy reporter was posing Mom and Dad by the table and the big box of food. "Hold up that box of oatmeal and smile," he ordered. "Good! People like to know their donations are appreciated, you know."

Katie jerked her nose back when Joe posed Hannah and Alex in front of the tent. She heard the crackle of paper. "Hey, a chocolate bar!" exclaimed Alex.

Chocolate! Without thinking, Katie poked her head out the canvas door and blinked in the camera's blinding flash. When she could see again, Katie burst from the tent. "Don't you dare put my picture in the paper!" But a grinning Joe was already loading his gear back into the wagon.

He hopped back in his car and leaned his head out the window. "Don't worry, young lady. Everything will be just fine. It's been a pleasure to meet and talk with you folks. My article should be in the paper in a few days. I'll be sure and bring you a copy. I have a feeling we can expect great things from this article." Joe the reporter disappeared in a flurry of dust, smoke, and engine backfires.

⌒

Dark, heavy rain clouds hung over Crooked Bend Campground, threatening a downpour at any time. Katie's heart felt as heavy as those clouds. Most of the time she hoped Joe's article would never be printed in the paper. She also knew Dad thought a newspaper article might be their best hope of getting job offers before fall and winter set in.

Three more families had pulled up camp and left Crooked Bend, including Alex's friends with the little hound dog. Several other families were planning to stay for the winter. What would the Barnes family do?

Dad and Mom spent a lot of time having private talks. One night, Katie lay in her sleeping bag inside the tent and listened.

"I'll tell you, Sarah," said Dad, above the crackling embers of the dying campfire, "I'm about ready to pull out of here. If we just had the money I'd load this van and head right back to Kansas."

Mom murmured something. Katie huddled in bed and crammed her fist against her mouth so she wouldn't cry. *It's all my fault,* she thought. *If only I'd taken better care of the chest, we'd have money to go back home now.* "Oh, God," she whispered, "if you can hear me at all, please help me find Gwen Van Switt and my grandma's chest. We've got to get back home."

Beside her, Hannah began a hacking cough, and across the tent Alex snored. Katie heard the sizzling sound of wet coals as her mom and dad put out the fire before coming to bed.

Four days later Joe showed up again, his white station wagon careening to a stop beside the van.

"Hey, it's Joe!" shouted Alex when the dust cleared.

Joe came loping toward them, waving a newspaper over his head. "Look at this, everybody!" A toothy grin flashed through his scraggly beard. "We made the front page of the *Mapleton News!*"

Mom, Dad, Alex, and Hannah clustered around to view

the open newspaper. "Oh, my!" gasped Mom. Finally, her curiosity got the best of Katie once more. She joined the others and stretched to peek over Hannah's head.

"I Was Hungry and You Fed Me!" read the big headline. Underneath was a picture of Mom and Dad holding up cans from the box of groceries. Below the written article was another picture, this one showing Hannah and Alex posed in front of the tent, their mouths rimmed with chocolate. Horror of horrors, above them, Katie's head poked through the tent opening, her eyes and mouth wide open in shock.

Katie staggered back and slumped down on her bench. "I will never, ever, set foot in Mapleton," she vowed. "That picture is the most humiliating thing that has ever happened to me."

"Aw, come on," coaxed Joe. "Hey, I already got good news for you folks."

Chapter Fourteen

"*A* job!" Alex shouted.

"Well, no." Joe's smile faded a little. "But the next best thing. I have a place for you to stay in Mapleton." He brushed fir needles from a bench and sat down. "See, there's this nice lady in town, Mrs. Phoebe Phillips. She's a real do-gooder, and a fine, church-going lady, too." He smiled up at Mom. "Anyway, Mrs. Phillips read my article in the paper and called right away. She wants your family to come stay at her house."

Katie felt panic as she looked at her mom and dad.

"Well, I don't think—" began Dad.

"Wait!" Joe stopped him. "You folks would have your own apartment in the basement. There's lots of yard room for the kids. And I'm sure there's a few chores you can do around the place for Mrs. Phillips." Joe paused to take a steaming cup of coffee from Mom. "Thanks, ma'am." He sniffed the fragrant coffee, then turned to Dad.

Katie watched as Dad looked over at Mom. Mom's mouth was clamped tight. She shook her head and Dad nodded.

"We sure appreciate all you've done for us, Joe, but takin' charity, why it just wouldn't seem right."

"I understand, sir." Joe finished his mug of coffee. "But think about this a few days." He fished a card from his shirt pocket. "Here's my number. Just get to a phone and call me, and we'll set things up." He eyed Hannah. "You gotta take care of that little girl. Cold weather will be coming before too long." After shaking hands with all of them, Joe took off once more in his white station wagon, beeping the horn in farewell.

"Dad, I'm so glad you and Mom didn't take that woman up on her offer," said Katie. "You made the right choice."

"I hope we did," replied Dad. He felt Hannah's forehead. In a few minutes he and Mom put Hannah to bed in the tent. They spent the rest of the afternoon quietly talking.

Katie and Alex went for another stroll. There wasn't much going on in camp. "I wouldn't mind leaving here," said Alex. "It seems like you'd want to move into town, Katie. You're so anxious to go to school and all."

"Not in Mapleton." Katie shuddered. "What would the kids in town think of us after that horrible newspaper article and pictures?"

"Yeah." Alex grinned. "I kind of wish I'd at least wiped the chocolate off my face before Joe took the pictures."

"We'd better get back to camp!" Katie looked up at the dark gray sky. "That rain's gonna come any time now."

By supper time sprinkles had begun, turning into a downpour through that night and the next day. The inside of the tent and the family's sleeping bags became soaked, and they spent most of the night huddled uncomfortably in the van.

When Katie woke the next morning and stepped out of the van, she wasn't surprised to see the wet tent already down.

Mom and Dad were packing and loading the top of the van. Fear squeezed her heart. "We're moving to Mapleton, aren't we?" she said.

Dad brushed water from his eyes and looked down at her. "Sorry, honey. There's nothing else we can do. Hannah's bronchitis is getting worse. We've got to get her someplace warm and dry." His face looked old and tired.

"I know." Katie shivered in the drenching rain. "It'll be OK, Dad."

When everything was finally loaded, they only stopped long enough to tell Shorty Jackson good-bye.

Shorty came out to the van wrapped in heavy rain gear. "It's sure been a blessing to have you folks up here," he said. "I'm glad you found somewhere warm and dry to move to, though." His smile was the only sunshine on that dreary day. "I wanted you all to know we're going to go on having Bible studies up here, thanks to your example."

"That makes it all worthwhile, Shorty," replied Mom, smiling back at him.

⌒

Clickety-click, clickety-click droned the windshield wipers, pushing streaming rain from the window. Dad leaned forward and strained to see ahead down the mountain road.

He stopped when he came to the little service station. "I gotta make a call to Joe." He wasn't gone long.

Clickety-click, clickety-click. The sound gave Katie a headache. Her shoulder felt numb where Hannah leaned against her and dozed, struggling to breathe through a stopped-up nose. As they left the hills, the tall green forest slowly disappeared, and the first houses came into view.

When they came to a green and yellow service station, the van slowed and turned in. Katie straightened up. "Hey, isn't that Joe's car?"

Dad pulled the van up beside Joe's white station wagon. "Yes. He's going to lead us to Mrs. Phillips' house." Joe was leaning outside his window, signaling them to follow him.

The wipers went on clicking, but the rain was lighter now. The van slowed as they drove through Mapleton's tidy business district: Ben Franklin's, J.C. Penney's, Hank's Hardware.

Still following Joe, they started up a hill, passing a huge brick church with a white steeple. The houses were getting larger, with big yards and spreading trees.

Finally, the station wagon signaled a right turn, and they followed Joe's car down a winding paved driveway with tall leafy trees on either side. As the driveway widened, Joe pulled up at an enormous white house with white columns in front.

"Wow, it looks like Scarlett O'Hara's southern mansion," said Katie. "And me without my hoop skirt!"

"It looks like we're in Snobsville, if you ask me," Alex muttered.

Mom looked back at them. "You two hush and behave yourselves," she said as the van stopped behind the station wagon.

"Well, this is it," said Dad, opening his door. As they all climbed out, they watched a woman coming out of the big house to meet them. She was very thin, wearing a flowing lavender flowered dress. As if on signal, the rain stopped and the woman tripped gracefully across the wide porch, down the steps and front walk.

"Welcome!" She flung her thin arms wide. "I am Phoebe Phillips, and I want to welcome you to my home!"

Katie heard the snap, snap of Joe's camera as he took pictures of Mrs. Phillips.

"How about everybody getting in this picture?" suggested Joe.

"Not me." Katie stepped aside. She was not going to be any part of these charity pictures. All at once she felt long bony fingers pressing hard into her shoulder. She looked up into the smiling face of Phoebe Phillips.

"We all want to be in this picture, don't we, dear?" Phoebe showed a lot of large teeth in a broad smile.

Feeling like a boiling teakettle inside, Katie lined up with her family. Joe snapped shot after shot, then flipped open his notebook and scribbled. Soon, with a wave of his hand, he dashed for his car and vanished. Katie longed to chase after him and beg for a ride away from this big house—and from Phoebe Phillips.

Mrs. Phillips' pleasant smile faded when Joe left. She turned to Dad. "Please drive that old van out back and put it in the garage." She glanced around. "I don't want the neighbors— that is, I don't want your things to get any wetter."

While Dad was stashing the van out of sight, Mrs. Phillips gave the rest of them a tour of their apartment. It was a small, plain apartment with hospital-white walls, very little furniture, and not a single curtain or picture on the walls.

"Now, there's not a lot of frivolous doodads here," she said with a wave of her hand. "Just essentials. I usually let visiting missionaries use this apartment, and they aren't used to a lot of useless luxuries. And you know, those poor souls are so grateful, their faces just beam." She looked sternly at Katie and Alex. Behind her back, Alex smirked at Katie and crossed his eyes.

"Well, you certainly are kind, Mrs. Phillips," said Mom. She scowled fiercely at her two older children. When Phoebe Phillips opened the small refrigerator, Mom gasped. "Oh, you didn't have to do all this! Why, this refrigerator is crammed with food. How can we thank you?"

Mrs. Phillips shrugged her narrow shoulders. "Oh, the church ladies did that. It seems to give them pleasure to assist with my missionary projects." She peered inside the refrigerator. "Tuna casserole! Oh, dear." She strode across to the door. "Well, I'm afraid I must be going. There's plenty of hot water. I'm sure you'll all want to take showers." With her hand on the doorknob, she looked down at Hannah, then over at Mom. "The first thing we are going to do tomorrow morning, Mrs. Barnes, is take that child to the doctor. She looks sick to me."

Mom brushed Hannah's hair back from her pale face. "Yes, she has bronchitis. Two years ago she had bronchial pneumonia. But we don't have the money for a doctor now."

"Nonsense!" snapped Phoebe. "My doctor is a personal friend. I'm sure we can work something out. Be ready at eight tomorrow morning." She marched out and closed the door behind her.

"Whew!" said Katie. "Do we dare take a free breath now?"

"Now listen, kids." Mom stood in front of them, her arms folded across her chest. "I know it's not perfect here. But we'll be sleeping in a warm house tonight. We'll be eating a good casserole. Tomorrow we'll be taking Hannah to a doctor. Let's just count our blessings."

Dad stepped inside as Mom talked, and now he nodded his head. "I guess you guys know it's pretty humbling for me to take charity. I've always figured I could take care of my family without help. But God's still leading us. Everything'll be fine."

That night as Katie lay in the top bunk above Hannah, she remembered her parents' words. With a sigh, she closed her eyes. "Thanks, God. Tonight was good—the food, this dry bed, and the hot shower—especially the hot shower, Lord. It's been so long." She lay silent for a minute. It didn't seem polite to complain to God after all these blessings. . . . "But, Lord, we need a home of our own. Not charity from someone who calls us a missionary project." She snuggled down under the clean sheets. "Anyway, thanks a lot, Lord." She closed her heavy eyelids.

She barely stirred the next morning when Mom crept in to wake Hannah. "You and Alex can just sleep," whispered Mom. "Your dad and I will go with Mrs. Phillips to take Hannah to the doctor."

Katie nodded and went back to sleep. She might have snoozed until they got back if she hadn't heard her brother banging and grumbling in the tiny kitchen.

Yawning and rubbing her eyes, Katie searched through the suitcase that now held her clothes, until she found a fairly clean pair of shorts and a T-shirt.

"So what's your problem, Alex?" she demanded as she joined him.

Alex was standing on a chair pawing through the top cupboards. "Shredded wheat!" he growled. "It's the only cereal here. I'll bet Mrs. Phillips picked this because it tastes like straw." He jumped down with a heavy thud.

Katie grinned. "Shredded wheat's supposed to be good for you...." She looked out the window. "Hey, they're back from the doctor already." Forgetting the shredded wheat, the two of them dashed out the doorway and across the manicured lawn. A big, shiny green Cadillac was stopped in front of the apartment. Phoebe Phillips stepped out on the driver's side, then Mom. Dad carefully lifted Hannah from the back seat and carried her inside.

"Is Hannah OK?" asked Alex anxiously.

"She'll be fine," assured Mom. "But thank God we took her in this morning. The doctor said one more day of waiting and her bronchitis would have become pneumonia." Mom held up a small white sack. "The medicine alone cost a hundred dollars," she whispered. "We're truly indebted to Mrs. Phillips."

Their benefactor had walked briskly ahead of them, but she stopped to look back at Katie. "By the way, young lady, I have a church trustees meeting tomorrow night, so I'll drop you off for the church youth meeting. It's time you got acquainted with other young people."

"Oh, I can't," protested Katie.

"Well, of course you can." Phoebe disappeared around the corner.

"Mom, please," begged Katie. "You know how she'll embarrass me in front of those kids. And that newspaper picture! I can't go."

But Mom's mouth had that firm-set look. "You will go, Katie. You do need to meet the kids here in town. Besides, look at all Phoebe has done for us."

⌒

The next evening, the big green Cadillac glided smoothly down the road. Mrs. Phillips sat in the driver's seat. She looked very pleased with herself. Beside her Katie slouched, wishing she were back in Crooked Bend, the streets of Seattle, or anywhere else in the world but here.

All too soon, they turned into the wide parking lot of the same brick church her family had passed on the way to Mrs Phillips' home.

"We must hurry." Phoebe Phillips locked the car doors and sailed up the sidewalk with Katie trailing her. Katie saw strange kids everywhere—they were sitting on the lawn, leaning on the railing, or tossing basketballs at a hoop next to the parking lot. Katie felt her stomach churning.

Phoebe looked back. "Don't dawdle, Katie Barnes!"

"Katie Barnes?" croaked a nearby voice. "Hey, don't I know you?"

Chapter Fifteen

"*W*hat?" Katie turned and stared hard at a tall lanky boy with a face full of freckles. "Hey, I've seen you before! You're the guy I met a few weeks ago at Puget Sound Beach. Tim . . . something or other?"

"Reilly. Tim Reilly." He grinned and blushed right up to the roots of his carrot orange hair. "You started to poke the jellyfish, and I—"

"Oh, I remember." Katie felt her own face growing hot. "What are you doing in Mapleton?"

Tim laughed. "I live here. This is my church, and these are my friends." He tipped his head. "You know, there's something different about you, Katie."

Katie didn't have to explain about her haircut because she heard the sharp click-clicking of Phoebe Phillips' high heels and her even sharper voice. "Katie, are you coming? You know I have an important meeting, and I do want to introduce you to the right young people."

"I'd be glad to do that, Mrs. Phillips," Tim offered politely. "Katie and I met earlier this summer."

Mrs. Phillips drew herself up and sniffed. "I hardly think

your lower Mapleton friends would be satisfactory, young man."

"Whatever." Tim shrugged. "It's just that I saw Henry Schaeffer looking for you a few minutes ago. I'm sure the trustees wouldn't want to start their meeting without their chairperson."

Phoebe's long face twisted in thought. She slowly nodded her head. "Yes, I must go to them. Katie, you'll have to manage without me. But remember, I'll pick you up at nine." Without a word to Tim, she strode away.

"So it's *your* family that's staying with Phoebe?" asked Tim. "Those pictures in the *Mapleton News* were kind of fuzzy."

Katie groaned. "You saw that awful article?"

Tim's grin stretched his freckled face. "I deliver the local paper. I could hardly miss a front-page story." Tim kept looking at her. "*I* know what's different. It's your hair."

"I cut it. It's no big deal." Katie scowled. "Let's forget about my hair. Listen, Tim, please don't tell the kids tonight that I'm a charity case who's living at Phoebe's house, OK?"

Tim nodded. "Gotcha. Now come on, Katie. I'm going to introduce you to my friend Shad Emery." He hurried her over to a tall, well-built African-American boy who was walking along with a basketball under his arm.

Shad's grin lit up his dark face. "I'm not only Tim's best friend, I'm also his next-door neighbor. Anything you want to know about him—just ask me." The three of them stood and talked for a few minutes, then started into the church building.

"Hey, Katie, how's that cute little sister of yours?" asked Tim.

As they walked, Katie told them how sick Hannah had been. "But she's already getting better since she's been to the doctor. I just hope we'll be leaving Phoebe's house as soon as she's stronger."

"Yeah. I guess Phoebe means well," said Tim. "She just comes on awful strong." He held the door open for Katie. "Right now I want to introduce you to some more people and the best youth sponsors in the state of Washington."

Within a few minutes everyone in the youth meeting became a blur of smiling faces. Ed and Joan Kipper, the sponsors, a couple about Mom and Dad's age, were every bit as awesome as Tim had promised. No one mentioned the horrible newspaper article and pictures, or Phoebe Phillips.

When the lesson and business meeting ended, Joan Kipper and a committee of helpers started spreading a long table with cartons of chocolate, strawberry, and vanilla ice cream; sauces and syrups; bananas and cherries—all the ingredients for homemade banana splits. A hungry, noisy gang of teenagers snatched plastic bowls and began to dig in.

Tim and Katie joined a group gathered around Ed Kipper. "Say, Mr. Kipper, how's the Good Samaritan project coming?" asked one of the teens.

"Pretty well." Ed took time to swallow a mammoth spoonful of sweet, sticky ice cream. "We've got our options down to two choices. One group wants to sell Mrs. Foster's house. They'd like to use the money to install stained-glass windows in the church building. The windows would depict the Bible story of the Good Samaritan." He paused to dip into his banana split again.

"The other group," he continued, "wants to keep the house

and turn it into a refuge and temporary home for homeless folks. There really isn't any shelter for them around Mapleton."

Katie nudged Tim. "What is he talking about?" she whispered.

"When old Mrs. Foster died, she willed her house to the church," Tim whispered back. "It's right next door. She wanted it to be used to help people, so we're calling it the Good Samaritan project. The church is forming a committee to decide how to use the house." He scraped his empty bowl. "Let's go back for seconds."

"You go. I want to hear this," Katie replied.

A well-dressed girl across the room examined her nails. "I don't think we want homeless people right next door to the church. I mean, they're dirty, they stink, and they probably steal, too."

"And stained-glass windows would look so cool in our church," said another girl. "My mom is on the committee, and she said they're going to hire that famous glass artist in Seattle."

Katie forgot where she was and who she was with. Once more she felt like a boiling teakettle inside. "Windows?" She jumped up so fast, her metal folding chair tipped over onto the floor. "You mean you think pretty windows are better than giving poor people a hand when they need it?" No one answered her.

"Well, I know what it's like to be homeless," she went on. "My family's been homeless all summer, and we don't steal! We've had to sleep in our van or tent. We've had to spend our days walking the streets of Seattle." She angrily began shaking her finger at the silent group. "I've seen plenty of people worse off than we were. People sleeping in dumpsters or store doorways." All at once Katie remembered where she was. She clamped her hands over her mouth. What had she done? After a quick glance at the wall clock, she almost ran from the room.

As she sped toward the parking lot, she heard the familiar click-clicking footsteps behind her. "I was just on my way to pick you up, Katie," said Phoebe Phillips. "Did you get acquainted with the other young people tonight?"

"Oh, I expect they'll remember me." Katie was thankful for the darkness that concealed her face from Phoebe.

"Splendid! A good first impression is so important. There are some fine young people in our church—from excellent families." Phoebe unlocked the car doors. Katie silently climbed in and fastened her seat belt. Soon the softly purring motor took them down the road again.

"My dear friend Berniece lives near me. She has a daughter about your age," continued Phoebe. "They're visiting in Victoria, Canada, for a few days, so she wasn't at the youth meeting tonight. A wonderful girl." On and on Phoebe talked.

Katie just sat back in the soft leather seat, closed her eyes, and thought how she had shamed herself tonight. She could never face those kids again.

Mom was the only one still up when Katie got back to the apartment. She was sitting at the kitchen table reading her Bible. She looked up with a smile. "Did you have a good time tonight, Katie?"

Katie tried to speak around the big lump in her throat. "Mom," she finally blurted out, "can we please go back home to Sunnydale?"

"This is our home now, Katie. I've been sitting here thanking God that Phoebe Phillips invited us to stay with her. Hannah is so much better. Her fever's down, and she's hardly coughing at all. I hope there is some way we can repay all of Phoebe's kindness to us."

"I have a feeling Phoebe'll find a way," Katie muttered. She hurried into the small bedroom she shared with Hannah before Mom could ask more questions.

In the dark room, she changed into her nightshirt and climbed into the top bunk bed. She lay there listening to her little sister's quiet breathing down below. "I do thank you that Hannah's getting better, Lord," she prayed. "I just hope she gets well real fast so we can move on." With a heavy sigh, she turned toward the wall and tried to sleep.

She awoke the next morning to bright sunlight in her eyes and Hannah's saucy face peeking up at her from the lower bunk. "Wake up, lazybones!" said Hannah. "It's a pretty, pretty day outside!"

Katie yawned, slowly sat up, and stretched. Everything looked better today. As she pulled on her shorts and T-shirt, she sniffed. Hey, it smelled like Mom was making fresh muffins! She could hear Mom's and Dad's voices out in the kitchen. Katie opened the door a crack to listen.

". . . and poor Mrs. Phillips felt so bad when she realized we couldn't go to church with her this coming Sunday because of Hannah's being so sick," Mom said. "I promised her we'd go next week for sure, so she could show us off to everybody." She laughed softly. Katie almost felt better. At least she wouldn't have to face that church full of nosy people this Sunday. Hurriedly shoving her feet into her worn tennis shoes, she jumped down and snatched Hannah by the hand. "Come on, hon. Let's go eat Mom's yummy cinnamon muffins!"

The late summer sunshine stayed with them during the next week. Hannah was getting better "by leaps and bounds," as Dad put it. He had been hired for a few days' work remodeling the local food bank. He still managed to mow Mrs. Phillips' huge lawn twice. He and Alex were also painting her big double garage.

Mom had washed all of the first-floor windows. She spent most of one day baking fancy little cakes when Phoebe hosted her hospital guild. Phoebe had no trouble finding extra work for all of them.

⌒

The next week, on another bright sunny morning, Katie was down on her hands and knees in the dirt, weeding a purple and white petunia bed. She jerked up a weed. "Oh, rats!" She had accidentally uprooted a purple petunia.

"Hey, Katie, look at this picture!" said Alex from behind her. Katie looked over her shoulder. He was clutching a Polaroid snapshot of an ugly black puppy. "Isn't he cool?" asked Alex. "A lady down the street has six more just like him. They'll be old enough to give away next week, and she says I can have this one. I'm gonna name him Little Mike."

Katie straightened up. "Alex, you can't keep that dog here. Mrs. Phillips would have a fit!"

"Why?" Alex crammed the picture back in his pocket. "She's got this great big yard, and there's a neat dog house out back. You know Mom and Dad promised me another dog when we got settled."

"Well, we're not settled yet." She pulled a dandelion from the bed. "That mutt is not the kind of dog Phoebe would allow in her yard. You better tell the lady you can't have the pup."

"No way!" snarled Alex, clenching his jaw. "God'll help us find our own place by next week. I got more faith than you, Katie." He turned back toward the road.

The poor kid, thought Katie, reaching for another dandelion. She struggled with the flower bed until noon, then tossed the weeds into a trash can, washed her hands, and went back to the apartment.

"Are you finished with the weeding today?" asked Mom.

"Yeah." Katie sat down at the table. "Are we doing something this afternoon?"

"*You* are." Mom began pouring soup into the bowls. "Phoebe wants you to meet some of her friends this afternoon for tea. You'll have to dress up."

"Oh, no," protested Katie. "I'll feel like a freak in front of her and her snooty friends. Besides, I don't have any summer dresses but that old denim skirt, and it's too short." She stopped after looking at Mom's grim face. "OK, OK, I'll go shower."

Two hours later, her hair still damp, and wearing the too-short denim skirt, Katie slowly trudged up the front steps of Phoebe's big house and punched the chiming doorbell.

The door swung wide. "Why, Katie dear, how nice," said Phoebe in a sugary voice. "Come meet my friends." She led Katie into her gigantic living room, furnished in velvets, silks, and thick plush carpets.

They stopped in front of a woman and a teenage girl who were sitting on a long beige couch. "Katie, this is my dear friend, Berniece Stimson, and her daughter, Nichole." The pair managed tiny smiles as they eyed Katie. *There's something strangely familiar about that girl,* thought Katie.

Phoebe snatched her arm and tugged her toward another girl who was sitting far back in an overstuffed chair. "And this is Nichole's dear little cousin—" The blonde girl squeaked and jumped to her feet.

As Katie stared at her, she remembered the very first time she had seen these two cousins. She stepped in front of the girl. "Well, hello. Long time no see!" She thrust her sharp nose inches from the pasty white face of Gwen Van Switt.

Chapter Sixteen

"*K*atie?" Gwen's baby-blue eyes bulged. "What happened to your long hair? I never expected to see *you* here!"

Katie scowled. "I believe we have something more important to talk about than my hair. Right, Gwen?"

"Oh!" Gwen darted a quick glance over at her aunt and cousin. Suddenly she pushed past Katie, then raced across the living room and out into the hallway. The next sound was the slamming of the heavy front door. Her aunt and cousin perched on the couch with their mouths open like hungry baby birds.

"Why, what happened to Gwennie?" her aunt finally gasped.

"I'm so sorry, Berniece, dear." Phoebe Phillips' long sallow face had turned dark red. "I warned you that this girl had no proper upbringing." She grabbed Katie's shoulder.

"Young lady, what have you done this time?"

Katie didn't answer. She twitched her shoulder free from Phoebe's bony fingers, ran across the living room, and followed Gwen out the door.

Standing on the wide verandah, she shaded her eyes and

looked from side to side. There was Gwen, blonde hair flying, as she stumbled down the driveway toward the front sidewalk. Katie grinned. This would be a cinch.

She leaped down the stair steps two at a time, and cut kitty-corner across Phoebe's velvety front lawn. By the time Gwen reached the neighboring yard, Katie had caught up with her. She snatched a handful of the blonde girl's silky yellow blouse and pulled her to a stop.

"Hold it, Gwen! Where is it? Where's my grandma's little letter chest? I know you stole it when we were at Puget Sound Campground."

At first Gwen could only pant and shake her head. Her face was red and blotchy, and her blonde hair hung down in strings. "No, I . . . I didn't!" she finally burst out indignantly. "And let go of my blouse! You'll ruin it!"

Katie only jerked harder. "It was you, all right. You were the only one in the campground who knew I had the chest. Now admit it!"

But Gwen went on shaking her head and struggling to free her blouse from Katie's clutches. "Do you realize this blouse came from Nordstrom's?"

"So?" jeered Katie. "I guess if you want to save that fancy blouse, you'd better tell me the truth."

After a few more feeble tries to free herself, Gwen stopped. She sighed. "Please let me go, Katie. OK, I lied. I did take the chest. But I didn't mean to steal it. I just wanted to borrow it."

Katie let loose of the silky yellow material and stared into those blue eyes. "Borrow it? You expect me to believe that?"

Gwen's bottom lip hung down as she smoothed her

wrinkled blouse. "It was really your own fault, Katie. You were so selfish."

"Selfish!" Katie shook her head. Was she hearing this right?

"Yeah," continued Gwen. "You wouldn't even let me hold the chest. Then, on our last afternoon at camp, I saw your whole family going for a walk, and . . ." She paused.

Katie finished the sentence. "And you saw your chance. You went right into our tent, found the chest, and took it."

"Only so I could look at it." Gwen sniffed. She pulled a tissue from her white skirt pocket and blew her nose. "And it was so pretty, I thought maybe Mommy would like to see it, too. She wasn't feeling well. She had a hangover—uh, I mean a headache." She tucked the tissue back in her pocket. "On my way to show her, I heard Daddy honking the horn. I had to jump right in the car with Mother when I got back, and then we drove off. What else could I do but keep the chest, Katie?"

"Ever consider telling your folks the truth?" asked Katie.

Gwen stared. "Are you crazy? And have them think I was a thief?" She shook her head. "No, when we left Puget Sound that day I was afraid I'd never have the chance to return the chest to you."

Katie put her hands on her hips. "Yeah, well you almost got that chance before today. My brother and I saw your dad when you were camped at Crooked Bend, but before I could find you, your motor home pulled out."

Gwen looked puzzled. "Crooked Bend? We never camped at a place called Crooked Bend. . . . Oh!" Her lips quivered. "That must have been after Daddy left."

"Left?"

Gwen nodded. "On our way home to California, Daddy dropped Mom and me off here one afternoon to visit. Then he drove off in the motor home and never came back for us." More tears gushed from her eyes. "When he finally wrote, he said he was moving to the Fiji Islands and that he never wanted to see us again. He—he said we're too much trouble."

"Wow, I'm sorry." Katie almost started to reach her hand out to Gwen, then jerked it back. What was she doing? This girl had stolen the most precious thing Katie owned! She must be going insane! "Um, I'm really sorry about your dad, Gwen, but could I have the chest back now?"

"I'll get it. It's in my room." Gwen turned and trudged sadly up the walkway of a large brick house with white trim and shutters. "My mother and I have to live here with my aunt and uncle now. All our money's gone with Daddy, and we lost our beautiful home in LA." She disappeared through a vine-covered entryway into the house.

Katie paced back and forth on the sidewalk. So now Gwen knew what it felt like to lose her home and everything. *I should feel good that she can't go around with her nose stuck up in the air anymore,* she thought. But Katie didn't feel good. She only felt pity for this girl who had once had everything money could buy. Imagine a father who didn't love you or want to see you again. She might steal and lie, but Gwen didn't deserve that.

"Sorry I took so long." Gwen's hair was freshly brushed and her face had been washed. But Katie's eyes were fixed on the little wooden box she was holding.

"Here." Gwen laid it in her waiting hands.

"Thank you, God," Katie whispered as she once again

traced the carved oak leaves and acorns with her finger. "Please, God," she silently added, "let the money still be here." She felt underneath the chest and pushed the lever. Slowly, the secret drawer creaked open. A green bill floated lazily to the ground.

"Katie!" squealed Gwen. "That drawer is full of money! Are those hundred dollar bills?"

"They sure are." Katie smiled. "I guess you didn't know you stole two thousand dollars when you took this chest, did you?"

Gwen looked shocked. "No! I didn't; I—"

"Well, you two girls certainly spoiled a perfectly nice afternoon," said a new voice behind Katie.

She spun around and saw Gwen's cousin, Nichole, walking toward them. Her crisp beige skirt swished with each step. "Thanks to you, Mother is putting poor Phoebe to bed with one of her terrible headaches, and there won't be any tea this afternoon." The tall brown-haired girl stopped when she came to Katie. She eyed the little chest. "Gwen, doesn't that chest belong in your bedroom?"

Katie looked over at Gwen and waited.

Gwen's face turned pink. "Well, uh, it really belongs to Katie. See, she and I were friends this summer when both our families were camped at Puget Sound. I sort of borrowed the chest then, and now I'm returning it." She didn't look at Katie.

But Nichole did. She eyed Katie up and down, from her homegrown haircut to her worn tennis shoes. "So that's where I saw you. You're one of those gypsies, aren't you?" She turned to Gwen. "Really, Gwen, you should be more careful of the sort of friends you make. Now come on, we're going in the house."

But Gwen stayed where she was. "Not yet, Nickie. I want to talk to Katie."

Without saying another word, Nichole turned and swished into the large brick house.

"You'd better go, Gwen," Katie said. "You don't want to be too friendly with us gypsies."

Gwen sighed. "Don't mind Nickie. She's . . . Well, she's really cool when you get to know her. But I guess she's kind of a snob sometimes.

"You're not still mad about the chest, are you?" Gwen continued. "We're still good friends, aren't we?"

"No, I'm not mad anymore about the chest. I'm just glad you gave it back and that the money's still there." Katie took a step backward. "Now about us being such good friends, Gwen . . ." Katie stopped. She'd been ready to repeat for what seemed like the hundredth time that the two of them were not and never would be friends.

She looked into Gwen's eager face. Maybe she could try. Maybe friends didn't have to be alike or agree on everything. Maybe sometimes it was enough to just need each other.

"OK, Gwen. Friends," agreed Katie.

"Oh, we're going to have such fun, Katie!" Gwen said. "We'll have sleepovers and go shopping, maybe we'll even be in the same homeroom at school."

"Maybe." Katie tucked the chest safely under her arm. "Now, I've got to run so I can tell my family I found the chest again. Bye, Gwen." She turned and hurried down the sidewalk.

"See you later," Gwen called after her.

I should have told her we'll be moving away, Katie thought. *The two of us won't be having many sleepovers or shopping trips.* Katie's feet slowed. *Now listen to me. I'm starting to feel sorry I have to leave this girl who's been my enemy all summer.*

"Please, God," she prayed as she walked. "Send Gwen a friend. She needs someone. Maybe you could make her friend someone who can tell her more about you? I don't think she knows you very well."

Now that she'd turned Gwen over to God, Katie felt great again. She could hardly wait to show her family the surprise.

It didn't take long to find them. As Katie turned into Phoebe's driveway, the old brown van came chugging toward her. Family faces stared from each window. Dad pulled the van to a stop, and Katie hurried over.

"Hey, Dad, how come you're off work so early?" she asked as she climbed in the back seat. "And where are you guys going?"

Dad chuckled. "One question at a time, Katie. First, I'm not working because the job at the food bank ended today."

Mom looked back with a little V-shaped frown on her forehead. "And, secondly, Katie, we were heading out to look for you."

"Me? How come? You made me go to Phoebe's party."

Mom's frown deepened. "Yes, and from what Phoebe's friend told me, you didn't stay long. She said you chased her friend's niece out of the house and both of you disappeared."

Alex hung over the back of Katie's seat. "Now Phoebe'll probably kick us out of the apartment—thanks to you, Katie."

"Hey, don't lay a guilt trip on me, Alex. Wait until you hear my news!" Katie leaned forward. "Mom, Dad, would you believe that girl who ran out of Phoebe's house was Gwen Van Switt? Phoebe's friend Berniece is Gwen's aunt. The only reason I chased after her was to ask about the little chest. And look!" She held the chest out to Mom.

"It's Grandma's chest!" squealed Hannah.

"Praise the Lord!" said Mom and Dad in chorus.

Katie beamed. "Press the lever underneath it, Mom."

Her mom reached under the chest. "Is all the money still here?" she asked.

Katie gulped and sat back. "You knew about the money and the secret drawer all along?"

"No, only since we got a letter from Grandma today. She asked if you'd found the money yet." Mom pressed the lever and the drawer opened again.

"See? There's two thousand dollars in there!" said Katie excitedly. "And Grandma's note says it's for us. We can go back home. Dad, I heard you and Mom talking the other night about wanting to go back to Sunnydale. Now we have enough money for the gas."

Dad smiled at her but shook his head. "Honey, that's the money your Grandma's been saving to get her roof fixed. It's the same money she tried to give us before we left Sunnydale last spring. I told you we can't take that money."

Mom carefully took all the bills from the chest and tucked them in a zippered compartment in her big purse. "Katie, you'll find that even grownups' faith wavers a bit sometimes. But your dad and I are finally beginning to see how the whole summer's been like one big answer to prayer. I expect you'll soon love living here just as much as you did in Kansas."

"No, I won't," said Katie. "We're never really going to belong out here in Washington. I'm not even sure God listens to our prayers out here. All summer I've been praying that we could move back home where we belong, but that sure hasn't happened."

"Why, Katie Barnes," scolded Mom. "How can you look at your little sister and say God doesn't answer our prayers?"

Hannah looked up at Katie and smiled. "I'm almost well now, Katie. God made me better."

Katie had to admit Hannah wasn't coughing as much. She tried to smile back. "I'm glad, Hannah."

"Now, folks, time to get rid of these glum faces." Dad turned and started up the van. "I'm going to take you all down the valley and show you a surprise that I think will make you smile."

Katie climbed slowly into the car. She folded her arms, leaned back, and sulked. What had seemed to be her best day all summer had become the worst. Now they would never move back home again. They'd go right on living homeless like a family of gypsies.

As they neared Mapleton, she resentfully watched passing service stations, fast-food places, and finally the downtown. This place would never be home to her.

After driving through two blocks of downtown stores, they came to a neighborhood of small older houses with tiny yards. "Who'd want to live here?" grumbled Katie. The houses were becoming shabbier and the streets full of potholes. They came to the end of the Mapleton city limits. Now there were fewer houses, interspersed with weed-clogged empty lots.

Alex poked her in the back. "So, Katie, are you gonna do it?" he whispered.

"Do what?" she hissed back.

But Alex didn't answer as the van slowed, made a right turn, and stopped.

"Why are we stopping here?" he asked.

Dad just chuckled as he swung his door open and stepped out. Mom quickly followed. Hannah and Alex excitedly shoved past Katie and out the back door.

Katie followed slowly. She looked around. All she saw was an old, sagging empty house, the kind that reminded her of scary stories. Boards were nailed across all the windows. Wild blackberry vines climbed the walls almost up to the eaves. Garbage was scattered everywhere, and the yard was a field of waist-high weeds.

Katie planted her hands on her hips. "So where's the big surprise?"

Dad spread his long arms wide. "Why, just look around you, honey. This place can be the answer to our prayers—a home of our own again!"

Chapter Seventeen

"*L*ive *here?*" gasped Katie.

"Yep." Dad climbed onto the rickety front porch. "This place belongs to my boss, Jack Kirby. He'll rent it to us real cheap." Dad crammed his hand into the front pockets of his jeans and grinned down at them. "No rent the first six months—if we clean and fix up the place a bit."

Katie looked at the spooky old house. "But, Dad, we can't. Your job at the food bank ended today. Remember?"

"That's the best part of my news!" Dad looked like he was about to throw his arms wide and start singing. "Jack Kirby says he can use me on his winter crew. We'll be remodeling an old grocery store, converting it into a minimall."

"Harvey, it's a miracle!" said Mom. "All we need to make a home of our own again is some of our famous elbow grease— some good, old-fashioned hard work. Right, guys?"

"Right!" shouted Alex.

"Right!" echoed Hannah.

Katie couldn't speak. She was waiting for Mom and Dad to laugh and tell them this was all a joke. That they would never move into an old dump like this. Instead, Dad reached in his shirt pocket and pulled out a key.

"Let's have a look." He twisted the key in the rusty lock. Finally the door creaked open. Stale, smelly air rushed out at them.

Mom and Hannah didn't care. They sped up the steps and followed Dad through the door.

Katie caught a glimpse of peeling wallpaper and torn linoleum. She planted herself on the bottom porch step. "I'll stay here," she announced.

"Poor sport!" Alex said and disappeared inside.

"I'm not a poor sport," Katie argued with herself. She just couldn't bear to be embarrassed any more. She wanted to go home and forget this whole summer.

The family's voices and footsteps echoed out the open door. It was taking them a long time to inspect that house. It was probably so awful that Mom would refuse to move in. "Please let that be true, God," Katie whispered.

At last Hannah danced out the doorway. The others followed. Katie's hopes rose when she saw Mom's grim face.

"I don't think I've ever seen a place in worse shape," said Mom. Katie felt like cheering. But when Mom spoke again, her hopes sagged. "But I think we can do the job. With hard work and God's help, we can turn this old shell into a real home."

"Yes!" Alex thrust his fist into the air.

Dad swept Hannah up in his arms. "Now, let's go see the back yard. There are a couple of old fruit trees."

"Oh, Daddy!" Hannah hugged him. "Can I have a swing? Please?"

"Say, isn't this my little girl who's been feeling so sick?" Dad perched her on his shoulder. "You bet. We'll find a good tree and hang your swing."

Alex trotted after them. "How about a dog? Can we get a puppy?"

Dad looked at Mom. She nodded. Dad's deep laugh rang out. "Well, son, Mom seems to think we can. You got a special dog in mind?" Their voices faded as they walked around the house.

Mom held back. "I'll be with you in a few minutes," she called. She sat down beside Katie. "You're not happy about livin' here, are you, hon?"

"Oh, Mom." Katie felt her voice getting all wobbly. "Everything's just so awful, and . . . and I want to go back to Sunnydale. I need my friends and school and church." She sniffed.

"I know." Mom put her arm across Katie's thin shoulders. "Your Grandma said your letters sounded really miserable this summer."

"Sorry," muttered Katie.

Mom gave her shoulder a squeeze. "She wants you to go back to Sunnydale and live with her. She said you could take bus fare out of her roofing money." Mom moved her hand back. "Of course, I told her you wouldn't want to leave the family."

But Katie jumped to her feet. "Oh, Mom, could I?" She clasped her hands together. "Please, could I go back home?"

Her mom looked surprised. "Why, Katie. Would you really want to leave? Your dad and I did talk this over, and we won't stand in your way, but . . . Well, you think about it this afternoon. Pray about it, too. Then let us know." Mom stood up. "Here comes your dad. Looks like he's found a box of something."

Dad's face was streaked with dirt. "Look here, Sarah. We

found four boxes of canning jars. There's an old cellar buried under blackberry vines out back. First thing tomorrow, I'll chop down all those vines."

"Wait, Harvey," said Mom. "First we'll pick all the ripe berries and can them."

Dad smacked his lips. "Lots of good pies and cobblers next winter."

Katie watched the two of them walk away. How could they be so happy about living in this old house?

Not her. She had the chance to leave, and she was going.

She turned and started wandering down the driveway. The weeds snatched at her skirt. Turning back, she looked at the old house. Yes, it looked as bad as ever. What would kids here say if they knew she was living in a house like this?

"Katie—is that you?"

Katie spun around. She shaded her eyes against the setting sun. Someone was standing at the end of the driveway. Someone with a bike. Tim Reilly! Why did he have to keep showing up in her life?

"What are *you* doing here?" she demanded, walking toward him.

Tim laughed. "Hey, I'm not trying to follow you. I was just delivering papers." He patted the empty canvas bag in the basket of his bike. "How come you're here? I thought your family would be headed back to Kansas by now."

Katie's face felt hot. "Yeah . . . well, my dad got a job in town, and my parents decided to stay in Mapleton." She looked back at the rundown house. "They thought maybe they'd fix up this old house." She clenched her fists and waited for him to laugh.

"That's cool," said Tim.

"Cool!" exploded Katie. "What's so cool about it? It's just an old shack in the worst part of town!"

Tim's face looked funny. "We like it down here real well."

"*You* like it? You mean you live around here?" Katie groaned and clutched her forehead. "I'm sorry. I just figured all the church kids lived in those swanky houses on the hill."

"Nope. I live right down the block from here. Shad Emery lives next door." He started laughing again. "Don't look so embarrassed, Katie. You ought to hear what some of the 'up-hill' people say about us."

Katie frowned. "Like what?"

Tim kicked at a clump of weeds. "Like we should go to church down here, with our own kind."

Katie grew angry. "Your own kind? And what's wrong with your kind? Why, I'll bet you work harder than most of them."

"Yeah, that's what Pastor Miller says. He's trying to get more and more valley people to attend First Church."

"We'll just have to prove to those snobs that they're wrong," Katie said. "God's church is for everybody, and they need all of us."

Tim grinned. "I knew you'd be a fighter, Katie. That's why I'm glad your family's gonna move into our neighborhood." He hopped on his bike and looked up and down the street. "I'd better be getting home for supper. See ya." He pedaled across the street, then stopped. "I'll tell Ed Kipper you'll talk to the Good Samaritan committee, right? I just know if you explain what it's like being homeless, they'll go ahead with the Good Samaritan house." Without waiting for an answer, he pedaled away down the street.

Now what? thought Katie. *How can I tell Tim I won't be living here in his neighborhood? That I won't be helping them get a Good Samaritan house? That I'm gonna chicken out and go back to Sunnydale, where everything is simple and easy? Will I ever get back to Kansas? More and more things keep getting in my way.*

Her mind spun around in circles as she trudged back down the weedy driveway. Her family and this old house. Lower Mapleton and Good Samaritan project. Even Gwen Van Switt planning to be her friend. It was almost like God didn't want her to leave after all. She shook her head. That couldn't be. God wouldn't ask her to give up something she wanted so much, would he?

She stopped when she came to the porch. There was a creaking sound as Dad pried the last board off one of the front windows. The setting sun struck the glass. It made the house look lit up inside. Like a family lived there.

"Katie!" Hannah scrambled up the steps. "You left Granny's little chest in the van. I brought it to you." She thrust the chest at her big sister.

"Huh, what's she want that old chest for now?" scoffed Alex. "There's nothing in it." Hannah's lower lip quivered.

Katie took the chest from Hannah. "So the secret drawer's empty now? That's no big deal. We'll fill it again."

"Oh, so you're gonna strike it rich," scoffed Alex.

"No, we won't be able to fill the drawer with money, but we can fill it with other good things."

"Like what, Katie?" Hannah's big eyes shone.

Katie looked around. "Like new memories." She spied a straggly rose bush struggling to climb through the tall weeds and berry vines. A few small roses clung to the weak vine. Katie snatched a handful of petals. "Here, we'll dry these and put them in our drawer. They can be a memory of the first day we saw our new house."

Hannah's small hand dived into her drawstring bag of toys she was carrying with her. She took out a tiny, flat red rock. "Mama made me leave my rocks and cones when we left Puget Sound Campground, but I had to bring this one rock. Isn't it pretty? Can it go in the memory box?"

"It's perfect," Katie said. "How about you, Alex?"

"Ah, this is dumb," said Alex. "I don't go around collecting rocks and flowers." He turned, jammed his fists in his baggy pockets, and started walking away. His feet slowed, and he turned back.

"Here!" He shoved a dog-eared snapshot at Katie. "It's the picture of Little Mike. Mom and Dad say I can keep him when we move here, so I guess you can have that picture for the memory drawer."

"Where're you gonna put the chest, Katie?" Hannah asked.

Katie looked at the old house. "We'll set it in our bedroom where we can see it every day."

"You're not gonna do it then, are you?" Alex said. "You're not gonna leave us and go live with Grandma?"

Katie grinned at him. "Of course not, Alex. How could you ever get by without me?" Her grin faded. "And how could I get by without all of you?" She looked over at Mom and smiled.

Mom smiled back at her. "Welcome home, Katie."

Dad tossed the pry bar into his open toolbox and straightened up. "Now that we got that settled, let's go somewhere and grab a hamburger so we can get to bed early. We've got a busy day ahead of us tomorrow."

"A busy day?" Katie said. "Dad, if fall is anything like this summer, I'd say we've got one busy *fall* ahead of us."

Dad laughed. "I believe you're right, Katie. And I feel almost happy enough to start singing."

"Please, Dad, wait 'til we get in the van," begged Alex. The whole family laughed.

How could I ever have thought of leaving them? Katie wondered. She listened to Alex and Dad joke back and forth and watched her mom pretend to scold them.

Finally, with the chest clutched under her right arm and Hannah's hand clasped in hers, Katie said good-bye to their gypsy summer and followed her family out to the van and into their new life together.

**From *Between Two Worlds*
by LeAnne Hardy**

Chapter 1

"VARIG flight 27 for Miami with a stop in São Paulo now departing from Gate 2." The breathy voice on the intercom might as well have been a hideous cackle, the way Cristina Larson's stomach clutched. She did not want to get on that plane.

"*Não!*" Márcia drew out the Portuguese word in a long moan. She embraced Cristina, and soon both girls were sobbing. "A year is so long! You've got to write to me. All the time. Promise?"

Cristina nodded and groped for a tissue in her pocket.

"Tell me all about your birthday," Márcia continued. "It will be wonderful having your *quinze anos* in America!"

Cristina wasn't at all sure that was true. Her Brazilian

friend probably imagined that Rum River, Minnesota, was right next door to Disney World. Why did their year in the States have to be now? Why couldn't it be last year or next year—any time but the year of her fifteenth birthday?

"Come on, Cristina. I want to hug Márcia, too, and we have to go." Cristina's older sister, Bete, stood by her side.

Márcia gave Cristina another squeeze and kissed her on both cheeks, then she kissed Cristina's right cheek one more time. "For luck," she whispered. They both knew what kind of luck she had in mind.

Everyone hugged and talked at once. So many last minute things needed to be said, and not enough time was left to take turns. How Cristina wished she could stay! She hated good-byes, hated pulling up roots and going to America. It might be "home" for her parents, but western Brazil was the only home Cristina wanted.

Márcia's mother dabbed at her eyes with a tissue and gave Cristina an extra kiss for romantic luck as well. Cristina giggled despite her tears. She was sure *Tia* Dalva had no idea that the "luck" Cristina hoped for was the tall handsome son at her side.

Vicente's dark eyes met Cristina's, and he put his strong arms around her. Then he took her shoulders firmly and kissed her on both cheeks. Her skin tingled, and for a brief moment Cristina wondered how long she could get away with not washing her face. *Tio* Zé and Cristina's father hugged and slapped each other soundly on the back as they said their own farewells.

The voice on the intercom repeated the boarding call. Cristina picked up her carry-on bag. It was heavy with all the treasures she couldn't force into her suitcase, but couldn't bear to leave behind. Shuffling through the gate after Bete, Cristina stopped every few steps and looked back at her friends. The black tarmac reflected the heat of the Brazilian sun. Halfway to the plane, she stopped once more and looked back at the terminal. It seemed like she had done this a hundred times before. It never got any easier. Vicente had his arm around Márcia who rested her dark, curly head on her brother's shoulder and waved a last farewell.

"I hate good-byes." Cristina clenched her teeth and started up the steps to the plane.

~ ~ ~

The corridor of Rum River High School was noisy and crowded with strangers.

"What are you looking at?" The girl at the next locker glared at Cristina. Cristina snapped her mouth shut to keep from answering back and jerked her eyes away from the girl's tight neon outfit. Her cheeks felt hot, and she knew they were as bright as the other girl's top. The girl slammed her locker and swept away.

"If she doesn't want to be looked at, she shouldn't dress like that!" Cristina muttered. She rubbed her nose and shook her head at the stale smell of tobacco the girl had left behind. Then a horrible thought scratched at Cristina's mind. She glanced down at her outfit and looked anxiously around the corridor.

Most of her fellow students were dressed in T-shirts and jeans. Some were wrinkled; some merely limp. Cristina wondered if Americans had ever heard of ironing. Here and there one or two students wore loud, tight outfits.

Evidently it was some American idea of *bacana*—"cool" or whatever the "in" word here was. But Cristina wasn't impressed. She and Bete had stayed up late last night, carefully ironing their jeans so they would look good for their first day. It was nice not to have to wear uniforms for a change.

Cristina shook her blond hair back from her face and tilted her chin. She closed her locker, but the door didn't fit right. So she slammed it. She wished Bete were with her now, but the seniors' lockers were all at the far end of the school. Cristina wondered how long it would take people to learn to call her sister "Bechee" instead of "Betty." She sighed and arranged her face in what she hoped was a confident smile, then she stepped into the flow of students.

"Cristina!" At the squeal of her name, Cristina turned and was smothered in Lisa Connors's welcome. "I just knew it was you! I've been dying for you to get here. I'm so sorry I was gone for the weekend. I couldn't help it. My parents made me go to this stupid family reunion. It was so bo-oring!"

Cristina blinked twice. Lisa had been her best friend in fourth grade—the last time the Larsons had spent a year in the States. Their families had been friends since before the girls were born. Lisa wrote occasionally, and their parents exchanged Christmas cards. Their annual photographs showed how much the girls had grown. Lisa's letters sometimes made Cristina feel like she was a trophy that Lisa pulled out when it suited her. "I have a good friend who lives in Brazil," she could boast if someone's grandmother made a trip to Europe or something.

Lisa's gush of words came to a pause, and Cristina realized she was supposed to respond. "That's okay. I was busy unpacking and getting settled," she offered.

"Oh, never mind. You're here. I can't wait to introduce you to everyone. You remember Ann."

Lisa turned to a tall girl at her side with meticulously applied makeup. Her long, softly curling hair, a shade darker than Lisa's gold, was brushed in a style that looked odd to Cristina, but she wore it with a kind of confidence that said it must be "in."

"Oh, yes, I remember Ann," Cristina replied. How could I forget? The month before they returned to Brazil, Lisa went off with Ann and told her all of Cristina's secrets. "You aren't going to be here anymore; I have to have other friends," Lisa had explained, as though it were the most natural thing in the world.

Ann's lips pulled back to show her upper teeth. Cristina thought it was supposed to be a smile.

"Is that the kind of earrings they're wearing in Brazil these days?" Ann asked. Cristina had studied the Connors's last Christmas picture and made sure she wore a pair of large clunky earrings like Lisa had worn. Now she noticed that both Lisa and Ann wore long, dangling earrings that swayed gently when they turned their heads.

"Why, yes," she replied. She hoped her face wasn't giving her away by turning red.

"Oh, how cute!" Lisa crooned. "I used to have some almost like those."

"Come on, Lisa. We have to get to English." Ann sounded impatient.

"What do you have now, Cris?"

Cristina consulted the schedule she had been given in the office.

"Uh . . . I have English, too."

"That's great!" Lisa squeezed Cristina's arm and pulled her toward the English room. Ann joined them, her face unreadable behind her makeup.

Between Two Worlds is available at your local Christian bookstore or by calling Kregel Publications at 1-800-733-2607